OTHER BOOKS BY EMILY HINES

HISTORY & BIOGRAPHY

It Happened in Virginia, 1st and 2nd editions

Speaking Ill of the Dead, Jerks in Washington DC History

Myths and Legends of Virginia, 1st edition

Virginia Myths and Legends, 2nd edition

More Than Petticoats, 1st edition

Virginia's Remarkable Women, 2nd edition

Mapping the Old Dominion

FICTION

The Proposal

Callie's Choice

A Place to Love

The Christmas Dance

Voting for Love

Burnt Station (humor)

Shadows on a White Wall

The Castile in the Wilderness

The Prince and the Passion

Fortunes Way

SELF HELP

Till Death Do Us Part

MEMOIRS

East African Odyssey

Christmas Changes

Coffins

from

the

Congo

Emilee Hines

Published by Escarpment Press

Published in the United States of America by
Escarpment Press, Hendersonville, NC 28739

Escarpment Press
www.escarpmentpress.weebly.com
Indian Land, SC

Coffins

from

the

Congo

Emilee Hines

Dedication

This book is dedicated to my Kenyan friends and my colleagues in the Teachers for East Africa Project, who are still alive, and to those to whom we have said our final "*Kwa Heri*."

Preface

Soon after I arrived in Kenya in 1961 as part of the Teachers for East Africa, I met the manager of the Nairobi morgue and his wife. He told me about a method of smuggling part of the government treasury of the Congo—then a crumbling nation—out of the country in coffins sent through Nairobi.

I thought at the time that would be the basis for an interesting novel. Starting in 1970, I wrote *Coffins from the Congo* three times, each time trying to save bits and pieces from one manuscript onto the next. Finally, I threw away everything I'd written and started from scratch. This is the result.

Some of the conversations or the way of referring to people may seem biased, but, at the time, this was a reflection of the British colonial influence in East Africa, which was still evident. Within two years, Kenya would no longer be British, but would be a new nation. The British were leaving what had been a very pleasant life in Kenya, and were scrambling for where to go and what to do.

I have used many Swahili expressions, which were used mainly between Europeans and their employees. The term "houseboy" was used throughout East Africa to refer to an adult instead of "house servant."

The events in this book are the product of my imagination. The characters are either fictitious or a composite of several people I knew.

Chapter 1

Managing the last step of the pulldown stairway, I leaned against a rafter to catch my breath. My granddaughter, Shannon, was ahead of me, and was beginning to pull things out from under the eaves into the center part of our attic.

"I don't think there's anything here that we will be taking with us when we move," I said. "We can make two piles, one to donate and one to discard."

"I brought four bags," Shannon said, indicating the big black plastic garbage bags she had brought. "One for things to sell on eBay, one that I might like to have, one to donate or discard, and one for things you might like to keep."

"I've kept too many things too long as it is. As for the set of Christmas dishes and the Christmas tree stand, when was the last time we had a big Christmas dinner here or I put up a big Christmas tree? You and Jeremy are grown-up and have your own places and your own Christmas customs."

"Okay. So, donate. What about these strange carvings of skinny man with walking sticks?"

She handed me the set of African carvings, and I brought them to my nose. It was amazing that after over fifty years, the wood still had a distinctive aroma, and amazing that smelling one with that aroma could take me back to my time in Kenya.

"What's this strange-shaped thing that looks like a shield?" Shannon asked, breaking into my revelry.

"Most of us decorated our flats with what we considered traditional African things—shield, spear, carvings, and drums."

"Like this one?" She pointed, then picked it up and tapped lightly on the surface of its zebra skin top. Even after all the years, it still was taut enough to produce a slight sound. "Did you play it, Grandma?"

I laughed. "No, dear. I used it as a little table beside my chair, where I could set a cup of tea and a little plate with cake, or RT biscuits.

"Are you taking any of your African things with you to the Palms?" she asked.

"The copper tray from Zanzibar, and the ebony bookends carved like the heads of Masai warriors. I use *those* things." I looked around at the objects she had laid out.

"What kind of wood are those carvings made of?" she asked. "It smells good, but the carvings are ugly, with the figures all bent over and their ribs showing."

"They are carved from *Mvuli* wood. I don't recall ever seeing a Hooley tree and I probably wouldn't recognize one if I did. They were carved during a famine. It hadn't rained enough for three years to make the crops grow, so the people were starving. These carvings are symbolic."

"They don't look like anything that we saw when you and Grandpa took us to Kenya."

I handed her the carvings. She was right: the sculptures and all the souvenirs in the shops across East Africa were more sophisticated, much bigger, and vastly more expensive. Some of them were museum quality, but I hadn't been tempted to buy any of them. They wouldn't remind me of Africa as much as did an impoverished African tapping on my window as I sat eating lunch, holding up a carving and beginning to bargain over the price. Any money that he could get would be better than nothing. I handed the

2

carvings to Shannon. "They're yours if you think you can sell them on eBay or if you want to keep them yourself. I don't need them to remember that time."

But remember I did.

I saw that she was holding up some baby clothes. "Do what you like with those," I said. "They were yours."

"Are you going to urge me to marry Morgan and start having babies?"

I shook my head. "Don't be in a rush. Travel and have some adventures, and make sure that settling down is what you really want."

"Adventures like yours?"

"No, yours will be different. Times change, and places change. My adventures could only have taken place when they did." (I had never told my children, much less my grandchildren, the whole truth about my time in East Africa, and I doubted I ever would.)

Children and grandchildren never think of their elders as young and adventurous, even foolish. I pulled up a small stool, sat on it, and opened a box, lifting off the ceiling tape grown yellow and brittle with age. While my hands were busy, my mind flew back to when I was young and adventurous, back to the night when the trouble started.

1962

I sat at the dining table, in the house that had been Phillip's and mine and was now mine alone—always alone. The sun was slipping behind the Muwa hills. This close to the equator, there was no lingering dusk, only a quick nightfall, like a knife cutting off the day. The sky changed from blazing orange to orange and black stripes and then to only blackness.

The coffee farm was on a slope overlooking the small town. The European country club was brilliantly lighted, and I could hear raucous shouts and laughter and occasional singing. Beyond the hospital, in a part of town where I never went, were the Asian club and the African club. Whatever went on at the Asian club, it was quiet. Then the drums began at the African club—death drums—slow and throbbing like someone sobbing.

"*Kwisha, memsahib?*" my houseboy, Muyia, inquired from the doorway, asking if I were finished with my dinner.

I nodded and pushed aside my barely touched plate. "I hear the drums," I said. "Has someone died?"

Muyia had worked for Phillip's family for years, and spoke a lot of English. Sometimes if he didn't want to answer a question, he pretended he didn't understand. This time, he didn't pretend. Not meeting my eyes, he said, "Not yet."

I wanted to ask him more, but he picked up my plate and said, "Bad times come soon." He walked out to the kitchen, his rubber sandals making soft flops on the floor. I heard water running and then a click as he softly closed the back door and locked it behind him. Muyia feared the death drums. He believed that the drums foretold a death that affected him or me. Most Kenya Africans are Christian, but they still hold on to vestiges of superstition. If it were an African death, Muyia would be asking for a few days off so he could go with a dear friend back to the village where he had grown up for a funeral.

A European death would mean a service at church, a reception at the country club, and very likely the body would be shipped to the UK for burial. This was happening more often now that so many Europeans were selling out and leaving the country.

If the death were an Asian, we wouldn't know until the smoke began to rise from the funeral pyre by the highway leading to Nairobi.

I GOT READY FOR BED, but I couldn't sleep. The drums had predicted Phillip's death, though I hadn't believed it at the time. When I asked about them, Phillip had scoffed. "Maybe some African chief" he said, pulling me into his arms and kissing away my fears.

I met Phillip the first week I was in Kenya; he was one of a group of American teachers. The local Europeans gave a party at the club to welcome us and introduce us. He smiled at me, walked across the room to introduce himself, and I fell in love. A month later we were married and Phillip's parents deeded the coffee farm to him and retired to Malta.

Those were the happiest days of my life, teaching by day at the nearby college, and spending nights and weekends at the farm with Phillip. But they were all to brief.

FROM THE COFFEE WORKER'S HOUSES came the familiar odor of charcoal fires. The death drums kept beating, frightening and maddening. I put what had been Phillip's pillow around my head but that didn't blot out the sound of the drums.

I was busy and happy with my double life—by day, teaching English composition, and by evening dining with Phillip on our patio watching the sun disappear behind the Muwa hills, and then lying in bed in each other's arms, listening to the night sounds. The coffee workers welcomed us and celebrated our marriage by marching around the house that first night, shaking tin cans filled with pebbles, dancing, singing and beating on drums. These were happy times and happy sounding drums. Later I was to hear rain

5

beating on the tin roof of our house, refreshing the red earth around the coffee trees. Still later, I heard the death drums.

Some evenings, we'd have drinks at the club with Peter and Muriel, who owned the farm next to ours and if there were a rugby or soccer match on a weekend, I'd either be helping to prepare food for the players and fans, or riding with Phillip to somebody else's clubhouse to watch the match and eat the food their wives had prepared. One who often played beside Phillip was Marcello Bonetti, who sometimes joined us for drinks, and at other times played darts with the men. I could tell by the straight lines of Muriel's and Peter's mouths and the way they turned their shoulders ever so slightly away from him, that they didn't like him. Peter even brought it up to Phillip.

"He's an all right mate," Phillip said.

"Haven't you noticed the way he looks at your wife?" Muriel asked.

"Well, why not? Joanna's good to look at."

Six months after our wedding, when Phillip's parents ought to have been coming out for a visit, they came instead for Phillip's funeral.

Phillip had often shared the ride to the matches with Marcello but not that time. "He's not coming back this way after the match," Phillip explained. "He's going to Kampala and on to Kasese," he said. "He's been acting strange, and I think he's gotten involved in something dicey, but when I tried to talk to him about it last week, he pretty much told me to keep my nose out of his business. I wish you were coming with me, love."

"It's coming to the end of term," I said, "and I have a stack of exam books to grade and return to my girls on Monday morning. I'll miss you."

"And I'll miss you," he said, giving me a kiss. "My life is so much happier when you're with me." Those were the last words I ever heard from him.

I WAS GETTING A LITTLE edgy when Phillip didn't get home at the usual time. I saw car lights coming down the drive, and then there was a fateful knock at the door. Marcello came to tell me of Phillip's accident. Later, the police said my husband was dead.

The next few days were a blur. Phillip's parents came out from Malta for the funeral. Such a short time before, they had stood with us at our wedding reception, smiling with happiness. Now, we stood with tear-stained faces and eyes red from crying. Phillip's mother grasped my hand, and I could feel her tremble. He was her only child, and now there would be no grandchildren. She asked me what I planned to do.

"I still have a year to go on my teaching contract, so I'll stay for that at least. I can move back onto the campus if you want to sell the coffee business."

"Oh, my dear, it's yours to do with as you wish. Phillip left it to you." She drew me to her for a quick hug, then moved back and added, "Don't make any decisions right away. Any quick decisions you make while you're still in shock and grief will be wrong. I think you're wise to stay on and fulfill your contract. You're a young lady of integrity. If we can help you in any way, don't hesitate to call us. And, by the way, we've requested an investigation of the accident."

Chapter 2

After Phillip's funeral I managed to drag myself to the college until the school term ended and holidays began, along with the long rains. I sat in the lounge and watched the rain fall, blotting out the site of the clubhouse across the pasture, and even the little brown brick Protestant church and the bigger Catholic one. Muyia brought in my breakfast tray each morning, and I sent most of it back uneaten. Copies of the *East African Standard* piled up unread, until finally Muyia took them away to be shredded for mulch in his garden. When bottles of milk accumulated in my overflowing fridge, I gave them all to Muyia to take home for his family.

Coffee wasn't picked or roasted during the rains, and there was little for the workers to do.

Muriel called several times, inviting me for tea or for a shopping trip into Nairobi, but I declined, saying I wouldn't be very good company. My mother-in-law wrote worriedly that Muriel was concerned about me. She urged me to get out and mingle with people again. I laid the letter aside.

Then one day Muriel showed up unannounced, and marched in before I could get to the door. "Look at you! When did you last shampoo your hair and get dressed up, even in some everyday clothes, not a rag?" She strode into the bathroom, put the plug into the bath tub and turned on the water. "Strip off those filthy clothes and drop them into the hamper, then get in this tub. I'm going to scrub you down, and when you've dried off, you're getting dressed and I'm taking you to the club. People have been asking about you. Have you even noticed that the rain has stopped?"

While she sudsed my hair and poured a pitcher of warm water to rinse it, she kept talking. "School starts again next week, doesn't it? Aren't you planning to teach?"

"I have to," I said.

An hour later, she drove us to the clubhouse, where a rugby match was in progress. Without asking, she ordered me a gin and tonic, and the waiter brought our drinks along with a little bowl of peanuts, or groundnuts, as Kenyans call them. It all seemed so normal that I could almost imagine Phillip out there playing along with his mates.

One by one, the players came by to express their sympathy, and say how much they missed Phillip. I could barely hold back my tears, but I knew this was important to them and I had to go through with it. I made myself smile and say something to each of them.

The last was Marcello, who didn't mention Phillip, but walked up with Muriel's husband, Peter, and asked with a smile, "May I join you?"

I looked from Marcello to Peter to Muriel, and saw they were waiting for me to answer. "Yes, of course."

The two men, sweaty from their rugby match, sat down and waved to the now busy waiter to bring over the beers for themselves and the second drink for Muriel and me. I had finished my gin and tonic without realizing it.

When someone put a record on the record player, Marcello asked me to dance, and when we'd danced only a few moments, other players began to cut in—Phillip's former teammates—and it was as if they were welcoming me back to society, which in a way they were.

When I returned to the table, Marcello asked, "How would you like to go into Nairobi to the cinema and have dinner?"

Before I could answer, Muriel said, "What a grand idea. Of course, you should go, Joanna. Let's make it a foursome, shall we? We've hardly left the house during all this rain."

So, it was decided, without my saying a word, and it became the pattern for most weekends during the next few months. We went to sporting events, a play at the Donovan Maule theater, the Lobster Pot, the Jacaranda Tree, and other restaurants, and to the horse races, where I won a few shillings.

Marcello was always pleasant and charming, and even Muriel had no real complaints, except to say, "I mistrust men who are too charming. I always wonder what they're after, and I usually know. Be careful of him, Joanna."

Marcello and I were seen at the club with Muriel and Peter so often that people began to consider us a couple, and no other teammates of Phillip's asked me out. I realized that I had drifted into a relationship without a conscious decision, but it was pleasant to go out in company and not sit around the house alone listening to the drums.

Marcello showed up at my house one afternoon bearing a bouquet of flowers in one hand and a bottle of wine in the other. "Your mother hen has protected you long enough," he said. "I have come to court you all by myself, and that's the way I want it from now on."

"These roses are lovely," I said, arranging them in a vase.

"They came from my own garden. On Sunday night I will take you to see it, and cook you a good Italian dinner — just you and nobody else."

ONE NIGHT, A WEEK OR so later, Marcello showed up just as I was sitting down to a light supper.

"I wasn't expecting you," I said. "I'm afraid I don't have much to offer in the way of supper."

11

He waved his hand dismissively. "No matter. A bit of cheese and some bread to go with this bottle of wine will be enough for Marcello anytime."

I started to the kitchen, but he put a hand on my shoulder and pressed me gently back down to my seat. "Eat your food while it's warm. I know where you keep the food and the glasses. I have something serious to say."

We ate in silence and sipped our wine while the sun slipped behind the Muwa hills and darkness came suddenly. I had been living in Kenya long enough to get used to the suddenness with which night came, with no long dusk.

"Muyia, you come into the dining room."

"Memsahib?" he asked. He didn't need to say more. He had been with Phillip's family for most of his adult life, and a gesture or nod of the head told him that he was no longer needed for this evening.

Marcello waited until I pushed my plate aside, then stood, gathered our dishes and took them into the kitchen and put them in the sink. He came back and turned on the floor lamp beside the sofa. I closed the curtains, but if anyone had wanted to see in, they could easily have looked through the glass-paneled front door.

Marcello patted the sofa beside him and I sat down a bit uneasily. I hoped that he wasn't about to say anything romantic. I still wasn't ready for that. To my surprise, he said, "I am going away for a while—at least a week. I would take you along, but it is business. When I come back, I should have enough money to take you on a long trip, perhaps even to Italy or at least to the coast."

"Where are you going? Is it a secret?"

"No, actually. I want you to know. In case something happens to me, you will know where to start looking." He took a roadmap of Uganda out of his shirt pocket and spread it on the coffee table in front of us. "I lived in Kampala for a while, and I have a friend there. Franco is from my hometown in Italy. I will stay overnight with him." He pointed to something he'd scribbled on the margin of the map. "This is his address. You may also want to talk to Lisa. She owns La Quinta and she used to live in the Congo. From there I will go to Kasese, where I used to work." He traced the route with his finger, and then pointed to another address scribbled in the upper corner of the map, where he had drawn a star. "I may even go into the Congo."

I was startled. "That sounds dangerous," I said.

"It may be, but don't worry, sweetie *mia*. To make a big profit, sometimes you have to take a big chance. If, by any chance, you are going to Nairobi, stop off at my house and see what my lazy house boy is doing. Sometimes those chaps take a holiday when the master is gone."

"What is he supposed to be doing while you are gone?"

"Seeing to the garden and keeping the house clean, and maybe putting a cover over the papaya plants.

He took my hand, gave me a brief kiss and stood. Don't worry about me unless more than a week has passed." He stood. "I am doing this for you *and* for us." He held up his hand, his finger and thumb about three inches apart. "Do you love me this much?"

I held up my own hand, my index finger no more than an inch from my thumb. "Maybe *this* much," I said.

He laughed. "That is at least a start."

With that, he kissed me and left.

I sat alone, worried about what he was doing that might involve the Congo, and the implication that he was doing it for me. I got out a stack of exam books to mark, but I couldn't concentrate on the early explorers of East Africa. So, I turned out the light, made sure the doors were locked, and got ready for bed, although it was still early

I pulled the mosquito netting free of my bed, so I could slide inside, and re-tucked it.

I finally fell asleep, hearing the insistent drums and smelling the fragrance of the Frangipani growing just outside my window and the acrid odor of wood fires out beyond the coffee mill.

Chapter 3

The sun was just rising, and mist clung to the hills when I awoke and got dressed the next morning. The town was just beginning to stir, with a few lorries on the move. I heard Muyia in the kitchen filling the electric kettle and walking over to plug it in just as the Karmali delivery van arrived and pulled up at the back door. Muyia went to take in the *East African Standard* and a fresh bottle of milk, and to hand the deliveryman my clean, empty milk bottle with my grocery order tucked into its mouth. It was a normal day and I could almost forget the drums. They could have referred to anyone, or just to some bad news as Muyia had predicted. Marcello had been gone only a week, the time he'd told me he would be gone, so it was too soon to worry.

After breakfast, I drove over to the college, arriving just before 7:30, as usual. I'd spent the past week with end-of-term activities, the main one being collecting and sorting all the textbooks and storing them in the book room. That day, we had to inspect the dorms and bathrooms to see if they were clean and that none of the girls scant belongings had been left behind. Then, the girls, wearing bright, flowered dresses they'd made and cardigans they knitted, would board the buses and head for home. When the last bus had been filled and had pulled away in a cloud of bluish smoke, we teachers wished each other a happy holiday, and I was free to sleep and be lazy—or, so I thought. I still planned to call Marcello and find out where he'd been and what had happened.

As I left the campus and started driving back up the hill to the coffee farm, on impulse, I turned instead toward Muriel and Peter's house. It was about time for her afternoon tea, and I knew she wouldn't mind my dropping in unannounced.

She greeted me with a hug and led me into the lounge. "It's such a lovely day," she said. "Let's have our tea out on the veranda." It must have been ready, because her house boy padded out carrying the usual tray with the teapot, a pot of hot water, two cups, sugar cubes, a little pitcher of hot milk, and a strainer to collect the skim, as well as a plate of chocolate biscuits.

We sipped our tea in silence as I looked out at her lovely well-kept garden. Muriel finished her tea and set down the cup. Turning to face me, and studying me with the gaze that let me know I couldn't hide anything from her, she asked, "What's been going on? You haven't been to the club in over a week."

"School, mainly. It's a hassle getting everything finished up and getting the girls sent home. Then I have to make sure the coffee is being picked, now that the rains are over and the berries are ripe."

"Marcello hasn't been to the club either," she announced. "Dare I hope that you are finished with him?"

I shook my head. "He's gone to Uganda—on some kind of business, he said. He said it was better that I not know about it, so I didn't ask any questions."

She frowned. What kind of business would he be involved in? He's not in the Army or with the police, so that he has to keep his movements secret, and he's not responsible for looking up new customers for cement. He's just in charge of making it."

"I know. It sounded a little strange to me."

She picked up her teacup again. "Do you think he might be seeing another woman? Not every man out here who goes around without a wedding ring is single. "Would that break your heart?"

"No, but it didn't sound like that kind of trip. He gave me a map of where he's going and the names and addresses of people I should contact if he's not back by tomorrow."

"That *does* sound strange."

"I told him I would go and check on his house boy and see that everything was all right there, but I've been too busy to follow up on that."

"I suppose we'll just have to wait and see," Muriel said briskly. "So when would you like to go into Nairobi for lunch and the cinema?"

"Give me a day or so to catch up on my sleep and energy and to see what happens with Marcello."

As soon as I got home I called Marcello and got no answer.

THAT NIGHT, THE DEATH DRUMS began once more. As Muyia finished washing up my few dishes and came in to say good night, he asked, "Everything okay, *Memsahib*?"

"*Indio*," I said, though everything was not right. "I keep hearing the drums. Do you know if anyone in the village died?"

He wouldn't look at me, but said, "No, *Memsahib*."

Before I could press him further, he left. I locked the door, shut off the lights, and lay in darkness, listening to the steady beat of the drums, as insistent as the beat of my heart.

Perhaps Marcello is just busy at work, I told myself. As soon as it was light, I tried calling him again. When he didn't answer, I got dressed.

17

I had slept fitfully, and couldn't rid myself of my worries. I knew something was wrong. I called Marcello's number once more, and again got no answer. He wouldn't have gone to work that early and should have been at his house. What if he was sick or injured and couldn't get to the phone? I had to go check on him.

After I gave instructions to the manager of the coffee farm, I drove toward Marcello's house *Athi*. When I turned out onto the highway beyond Talent, I saw that no fresh wood had been piled on the funeral pyre, so the death was not to be an Asian. I wasn't sure they believed in the superstition of the drums anyway.

What bad things were going to happen besides a death? Hadn't enough bad things happened?

When I first arrived, Kenya was in the third year of drought and some skulls and bones still lay in pastures where cattle and wild animals had fallen and died from starvation and thirst. When the rains came, they became a flood, washing away roads and bridges and marooning us for a while. Then came a plague of locusts, which crunched underfoot as I walked to class. They were followed by a plague of small frogs—not much bigger than a shilling—that died with a squish instead of a scrub crunch. Worst of all were the Safari ants that moved in columns of millions. They devoured larger insects and small animals, and could strip the berries and leaves off a coffee tree within minutes.

So, what else did I have to fear?

When I parked in front of Marcello's house and got out, I knew for sure that something was wrong. His car was gone, and an eerie silence met me.

The front door was unlocked, as I knew it would be. Marcello never locked his house, and lived simply, keeping nothing of much value. He trusted his servant to guard the house while he was gone.

"Marcello?" I called quietly. My voice was low, and in keeping with the silence of the house. No answer. I pushed the door wider, and saw Kilonzo lying in a pool of dried blood, his face so battered I wouldn't have recognized him, and his eyes swollen shut. He was wedged against a table leg, one arm lying uselessly beside him, as if he had tried to pull himself up or perhaps tried to crawl. I ran and knelt beside him, bringing my face close to his. "It's Joanna," I said. "Where is the Bwana?"

"Juana call . . ." He slowly whispered a number, and I tried to memorize it. ". . . Bwana."

"I'll get help for you, Kilonzo."

I called the police and told them that a badly injured man was in the assistant manager's house at the cement plant. I hung up quickly before they asked my name.

Kilonzo attempted to raise his hand to let me know he understood. I dialed the number he'd recited, and it was answered by a voice that said "Nairobi morgue."

Emilee Hines

Chapter 4

Surprised, I hung up. I was sure I'd heard the number right. I'd go there, and not ask for information over the phone.

I had just turned out of the street onto the road toward Nairobi when the ambulance came toward me. It was a close call. I'd done all I could for Kilonzo, and I didn't want to be questioned by the police, since I had no real information, only a phone number. As I parked in front of the morgue, a dark-haired woman got in a Volkswagen and drove away, narrowly missing me.

The morgue manager was a well-dressed Indian who greeted me in English. "Good morning, Madam," he said, extending his hand. As I shook hands with him, I couldn't help noticing the ring he wore, a wide gold band that looked like a cobra with its hood expanded, and rubies for its eyes.

He drew back his hand. "What can I do for you, Madam?"

"I think the body of my fiancé may be here," I said.

He asked, "What is his name"?

"Marcello Bonetti," I lied. There was a look of surprise on his face that quickly disappeared. "There is no one here by that name," he said coldly.

I took a tissue from my purse and made myself sob, my shoulders moving and my lips quivering. It was easy, as I was near tears anyway, thinking of poor old Kilonzo. "May I have some water?"

The moment he left to fetch the water, I pushed open the door and ran into the back room, searching for Marcello's body. Instead, on the table, I saw a large box with Marcello's last name on it and shipping directions that left from Kasese and ended in Rome, with the weight marked as 200 kg.

The manager grabbed my arm, sloshing water all over me. "You are not allowed in here!" He shoved me into the lounge area.

"You said he wasn't here, and he is. I want to see him for myself."

"The coffin is sealed and, as you can see, it is already in a shipping container to be sent to his home for collection. Now get out. You have my sympathy, Madam," he concluded in a cold voice, "but it's against the law to open up a sealed casket." He pushed me out and locked the door behind me

I sat slumped over the wheel of my VW, too shocked and puzzled to drive. My heart told me Marcello was not dead, but someone was using his name to ship a body out of the country. Marcello would never have had his body sent to Rome. He was from Portogruaro, a small town in Italy near Venice. And 200 kg. was an incredible weight. Marcello weighed perhaps 80 kg. Who—or *what*—was in that box? The authorities would not open a coffin, so long as there was a death certificate to accompany it, and maybe not even *without* a death certificate—or with a forged one.

Deep in thought, I had driven a good distance before I realized that a blue Peugeot was following me. *I must be mistaken*, I thought. *There's no reason anyone should be following me.* Yet, by the time I had passed the second roundabout and was on my way toward the Athi River and home, there was no mistake. Several times, the Peugeot had dropped back and let a vehicle or two come between us, but now it was bearing down on me. I sped up, and, as we approached the road to the airport, I saw in the rearview mirror that the driver had a pistol in his hand and it was pointed at me. In that same moment, a shot rang out and a bullet shattered my outside mirror. I sped up, and, with relief, saw that the Peugeot had turned onto the airport road.

Behind the Peugeot was a police Land Rover, which signaled me to stop. I pulled over, and a tall blonde man in khakis came up to my car. I recognized him from Phillip's funeral, as well as several social occasions at the club. It was Ian Armstrong. This was the first time I had seen him in a police uniform.

My hands were shaking on the steering wheel, and before he could say anything, I demanded, "Did you see what that driver did?" I indicated the shattered mirror. "He could have killed me! Why aren't you going after him?"

"I did see, and I radioed for someone to pick him up. We've been watching him for a good while, hoping he would give us a good reason to pick him up, and firing into an occupied vehicle is an excellent reason. And yes, he could have killed you if he'd wanted to. Your head is a bigger target than that little mirror, so my guess is he only wanted to scare you. Do you know why he might want to scare you?"

I shook my head. "No. I've never seen that car or driver in my life."

"And why were you at the morgue?"

"How long have you been following me?" I asked in surprise.

"Long enough. It's an unusual place for a young woman to go without some special reason."

"Marcello is missing, and I thought he might have had an accident and been there, unidentified. But he wasn't," I finished defiantly.

"What is he to you? Are you involved in some scheme of his?"

"He was Phillip's friend, and he's *my* friend. He's helped me through my grief over Phillip's death, that's all"

23

"I'm very sorry about Phillip's death. He was a good mate on the field. We may be calling on you to sign a complaint against your assailant, although my witnessing the event should be enough so we don't have to bother you. Follow me to the police station," he said.

"Are you arresting me?" This was getting stranger and stranger."

"No, but I want it to look as if I am. We need your help. Right now, you know more than anyone else where Marcello might be."

"Then you don't think he's dead, either?"

"No, not yet."

"Then who is in that coffin I saw at the morgue?"

"Don't argue so much, people will surely notice, and that will ruin our plan. Just follow me and I'll tell you all we know." He stalked off, got into the police vehicle and drove off. I followed him.

At the station, he led me to a small room that I assumed was ordinarily used to question suspects. I began to *feel* like a suspect. Could I trust him?

He had tea brought in, and I picked up my cup with shaking hands to take a sip, and waited for him to speak.

He set down his cup and looked at me with a bland expression and a slight smile that gave away nothing. "We think Marcello is responsible for Phillip's death," he began.

I gasped. "I don't believe it. He was Phillip's friend."

"Phillip's mother believes it. She asked us to investigate, and there's so much crime going on that we had little time to work on what might also be a crime. Phillip called me about an hour before his fatal accident, and said he had some important information for me. Unfortunately, I wasn't in, and he left a message. By the time I came back on duty the next morning and got the message, Phillip was dead. We were only a few weeks into the investigation when there was a flair-up in the tribes at the northern frontier and I was sent there."

I felt tears sliding down my face, and I couldn't say anything.

"The other reason we were looking for him has to do with those coffins in the morgue."

"Coffins? You mean there're more?"

"As a routine matter, we check who's in the morgue, and of course when we investigate a suspicious death, we take the corpse to the morgue. It was on one of those trips that I first noticed a coffin—or rather a shipping crate containing a crudely made coffin—coming from the Congo and being sent to Cairo. We arranged through customs there to seize the box and open it. To their surprise and ours, it held no body, but only pieces of lumber to approximate the weight of an average African man. We held up the shipment long enough to get one of our men in place in Cairo. Then, Customs delivered it to the person it was addressed to, and our man followed him. He opened the box, and didn't seem surprised at the contents. We were puzzled, but assumed it was a test to see if something more important could be sent by that route."

Ian paused to drink his tea, and then went on. "I began to take more frequent looks at coffins coming from the Congo. Every one was unusual, but the following week there was a second one, also addressed to Cairo. Despite the protests of the morgue manager, we brought it here to open and, lo and behold, we found another with the same Cairo address. This one *did* contain a body—a young African, crudely embalmed and still smelly—not weighing anywhere near the weight on the shipping case. It had a false bottom, and, hidden inside, we found bars of gold, very likely stolen from the treasury of the Congo now that the country has collapsed. We took out

25

half, sealed up the coffin and took the whole thing back to the morgue, assuring the manager that there was no problem.

"The Cairo police arrested the man who claimed the shipment, but not before he had sent a telegram saying: "Trial OK. Go as planned."

Ian stopped reading and looked at me. "It was sent to Marcello."

Chapter 5

I was too stunned to say anything. How had Marcello gotten involved in this? Was he to receive the gold in Rome, or was he going to be the next body that accompanied the shipment of gold?

Ian said, "When we belatedly went to talk to him about Phillip's so-called accident, he wasn't there. His car was gone and the house was empty, except for furniture and general household items. The door to his clothes closet stood open, but it too was empty. The plant manager said he'd gone to Uganda on a family emergency and had no idea when he might return, but promised to keep in touch." Ian shoved back his tea cup. "There you have it. So, we start in Uganda."

"We?"

"You want to find him, don't you?"

I thought about poor Kilonzo beaten unconscious. "Did you try to beat the information out of Marcello's house boy?"

"No, we don't get our information that way. The poor fellow showed up to check on the house and garden as he had promised, just as someone else came looking. We need your help. We'd like you to come with me, as a couple going on safari. Go home and pack a bag. Can you have a friend bring you into Nairobi? I'll meet you at the train. Pretend that you've been shopping and just barely made the train."

Without actually agreeing, I realized that I was now caught up in the search for Marcello, looking for whoever had beaten Kilonzo, and obviously something far scarier. "If we're going to be pretending we're a married couple on

Safari, I think I should know your full name and a lot of information about you, so I don't end up asking questions that a wife would already know the answers to."

"Ian Armstrong," he said. "I was accepted at the London School of Economics, but I had to do my compulsory military service before I finished my degree, and I was sent out to Malaya. I arrived back in London during the great smog and it took me seven hours to make my way home in the gloom, moving from lamppost to lamppost. I spent the next week cooped up with my mother and sister without milk delivery or a way to get to the grocers. When things cleared and the newspaper was delivered, I saw an advert for a job with the Kenya police, and here I am, where the air is clear and there is always something interesting to do."

As Ian escorted me back to my car, he said, "This adventurer of ours should be very interesting."

As soon as I finished lunch, I drove over to Muriel and Peter's. They both sat stunned as I told them everything that had happened during the morning and all that Ian Armstrong had described about the gold smuggling operation. Their drinks sat untouched until I finished. Muriel said, "I have mixed feelings about this. I want you to find him and confront him with what you know about him now. Surely you won't let him charm you into believing his innocence."

"Be sure you take Phillip's pistol with you," Peter said. "I'm just sorry you can't take his rifle, but that's too difficult to conceal. And rest assured that while you're gone, we will look after the place and see to the coffee picking.

"Are you taking Phillip's pistol?" Peter asked, and that question told me he'd given up trying to dissuade me from going.

When I nodded, he went on. "You know that if it's stolen and used in a crime, you'll be in deep trouble."

"If it's stolen, I'll already be in deep trouble. I'm going to keep it with me every minute I'm gone." I didn't tell them that Marcello had once asked to borrow it and I'd lied and told him I'd sold the pistol. I don't know if he believed me, but he didn't insist.

Muriel stood and clapped her hands together. "Well, let's get cracking. We're going to have to do some hasty packing for you and get you to that train on time. Be sure to get a good bath, Joanna, and use a bit of perfume so you'll really appear to be going with your husband on Safari."

People were already boarding the train, which sat chuffing in the station as we arrived. It was easy to spot Ian Armstrong, since he towered above the other travelers, resplendent in creamy white trousers and shirt, and a navy blazer. "Hurry along, dear," he said. "We've only got a few minutes to get on and find our car."

"It's my fault," Muriel said with a girlish blush. "I kept seeing dresses that would just be perfect for Joanna, and she kept telling me she already had enough things." She indicated Peter, who was laden with packages and a small suitcase. "You can see we found some gorgeous gowns for her, and I insisted she had to have her nails done."

I thought Muriel would have done beautifully as the star of a play at her girls school. I hugged her, took some of the bundles from Peter and left Ian to collect all the rest. I hugged Muriel and let Ian help me up the steps into the train. Once we were seated, I tapped on the window of our compartment to wave goodbye, and I saw a woman running across the platform and headed for the train. "I've seen her before," I told Ian. "I think she was driving away from the morgue just as I got there. She almost hit me."

29

"Don't worry about her, probably just a bad woman driver," Ian said.

I let that macho remark pass—for the time being.

"I assume you have a gun, and I, of course, have one. I doubt if she is involved in this smuggling ring." A shrill whistle blew, and the train began to move, taking us westward to Uganda. I patted my purse, feeling the map Marcello had given me—*and* Phillip's pistol. I couldn't help wondering if I would need them both.

Chapter 6

Ian stowed our bags, mine a very small case I'd brought over with me from The States. He sat down opposite me and pointed to the heap of what looked like the results of an afternoon shopping spree: some polyethylene bags with store names on them and others, heavy Manila paper bags with flat bottoms and raffia handles.

"Looks as if you and your friend, Muriel, made the most of an hour's shopping," he said. "Let's see what you bought."

I laughed. "Peter was urging us on to be sure we made the train with time to spare. Muriel took me to a beauty salon so I could get by nails done and have my hair cut and shampooed." I held out my hands with the fingers spread, and turned my head from side to side so he could see the results.

"Well done. No bride would be going off on Safari with her new husband without getting all done up. So, what's in the bags?"

I spread out the contents of the first bag, an emerald green, chiffon cocktail dress with a green, paisley print shawl.

He nodded. "We may well be dressing for dinner at one of the nicer hotels. The navy suit you're wearing is just right for train travel."

I said, "Your business attire is a big improvement over the khaki shorts you had on this morning."

He was wearing a tie that I knew represented some school. It meant a lot to the British, but nothing to me.

I opened another bag that held a pair of sandals, a pair of sturdy walking shoes, olive green slacks, a white T-shirt, and a beige cardigan I knitted myself.

"That's more like it," he said. "But when we get to Kampala, we'll be outfitted the way people expect to see Safari goers—especially newlyweds. What's in the last bag?"

"Night wear." I pulled out a fleecy bathrobe. "I learned my lesson the first time I went upcountry with Phillip and his family and found everybody having dinner in their bathrobes and slippers. I nearly froze." I hadn't decided whether to show him the nightgown and negligée, but he reached for the bag and gave it a shake. The beautiful white lingerie slid out onto the seat.

He picked up the lacey nightgown with one hand and the negligée with the other. "This really will make us look like a pair of newlyweds if anyone searches our compartment."

I stuffed the filmy garments back in the bag. "Muriel must have put them in. I wouldn't have brought them."

He asked, "Why not?"

"They were part of my trousseau when Phillip and I got married." His face reddened, and, after a moment, he said, "Forgive me, Joanna. I was about to make a risqué remark."

"Fortunately," I said, "I have some plain nightwear in my case," pointing to where he had stored my luggage.

He pushed the negligée and nightgown into the shopping bag and laid his hand atop mine.

"I'm sorry I said that. Although we have to do a bit of slap and tickle and act affectionate when people are around. Right now, I think we ought to freshen up and get ready for dinner. The conductor may wonder why we got two beds instead of sharing one, but the truth is this was all that was available at the last minute."

When the conductor came through to announce dinner we followed him into the dining car. Seated at the table, I placed my bag carefully on the floor, wedging it against the wall with my foot, and spread the snowy damask napkin across my lap.

"Joanna, my dear, would you like your usual?" he asked.

"No, I'm in a mood for a gin and tonic, please."

"I'll have the same," he told the waiter.

As we sipped our drinks, Ian said, "I forgot to mention that I had a note from Meg and Crickey. They want us to come out to the farm for a dinner after we get back from our safari. Crickey found an abandoned baby rhino and Meg has adopted it as a pet, giving it bottles of milk every day. She says he's ready for solid food, as he's eaten all her nasturtiums"

I laughed. "It'll be good to see them — and the rhino."

Food began to arrive in typical British fashion: leek soup, small fish croquettes and medallions of steak served with Brussels sprouts and broiled tomatoes. It was all delicious, but I ate slowly, postponing the time when I would be alone with him in our compartment. It was not until the waiter had brought sultana cake and small cups of coffee with hot milk that I asked, "Was there any other news you picked up this afternoon?"

"Oh, yes, I forgot. Kilonzo is recovering from his malaria and should be right as rain by the time we get back." He slightly emphasized "malaria" so I knew Kilonzo was recovering from his beating.

"That's good."

We both knew Kilonzo had been beaten close to death, and if he had malaria at all, it was purely coincidental. I picked up my purse, heavy with the weight of Phillip's pistol, and we made our way back to our compartment.

We both burst into laughter when we saw that our beds had been made up, the corners neatly turned down, and, on my pillow, the nightgown and negligée were spread out in readiness.

"I think we covered the drink situation very well. From now on, your *usual* drink will be gin and tonic."

"And you covered Kilonzo's situation very well," I said, "but who are Meg and Cricky? They sound very interesting."

"They're not imaginary characters," laughed Ian. "Cricky and I were in school together, and I was the best man at their wedding."

I took the first turn at using the bathroom and getting dressed for bed. I was on the cover in my plain pajamas when Ian came out of the bathroom. I had my back to him, so I didn't see what he was wearing to sleep in—if anything.

"Good night, sweetheart," he said in the darkness.

"Good night, dear," I responded.

"You may want to come up with something a little more romantic than dear," he said with a chuckle.

My mind whirled with questions and worries. Was Marcello involved with gold smuggling? That didn't really concern me. I was merely helping out the police, but I had my own reason for wanting to confront Marcello and make him tell me face-to-face the truth about Phillip's death. Who had beaten poor Kilonzo, trying to force information out of him that he didn't have?

In spite of worrying and having had coffee at dinner, the exhaustion of the day finally put me to sleep.

I was awakened when the train stopped with a jerk. I lifted the corner of the shade over the window by my bed, and saw the station sign that said Nakuru. I was about to let the shade drop when I saw a familiar woman step down from the train and walk across the platform: the woman I'd seen twice before, once near the morgue, and once running for the train. The platform was lighted so I could see her clearly, but a man who stepped out from behind a post remained in shadow. Only his hand and arm were illuminated, as he handed her a package that looked about the size to conceal a pistol. On his hand was a ring of a gold twisted cobra with sparkling red eyes, just like the ring the morgue manager had worn.

Ian was asleep and snoring lightly. I didn't awaken him, though I wondered if, when I told him in the morning what I'd seen, he might think I'd been dreaming. I let the shade drop as the woman turned back toward the train, and I had the uneasy feeling that she might have seen me watching her.

Chapter 7

Ian was awake and dressed when the attendant tapping on our door with the tea tray awakened me. While Ian drank his morning tea, I went into the bathroom and got dressed. When I told him what I'd seen, he said, "Do you think you could identify her if she is still on the train?"

"Yes. No question. And the ring as well."

"So we are beginning to see more people involved in this operation. There would have to be many, and that works in our favor. The more there are, the more likely it is that we can get information out of the minor characters and work our way up." He looked at his watch. "We'd better get breakfast and get our belongings together. We have a big day ahead of us in Kampala."

In the dining car, we faced the usual British breakfast: slices of rosy papaya with lime to squeeze onto it; slices of meat they called boiling bacon; fried eggs; baked beans; and marmalade and little balls of butter to be spread onto cool toast that rested in an upright rack. (I liked all of that, but I never could get used to having fried salted herring for breakfast.) The coffee was good and strong, and there was a pot of hot milk to go with it.

As we left the dining car, the woman I kept seeing came in, her dark eyes and dark curly hair contrasted sharply with her pale skin. She hugged her purse tight against the flowered dress she wore that stopped inches above her plump knees. Earrings dangled from her pierced ears, and a silver pendant on a chain hung in the cleavage of her breasts. She looked out of place even on a train in Kenya.

As soon as she had passed well beyond us, I leaned close to Ian and said, "Smile and pretend something's amusing. When the train stopped at Nakuru last night I saw her get off and take a package from a man. He was wearing a ring just like the morgue manager had."

"Maybe he's a friend of hers," he suggested. "Or it could just be coincidental."

I could tell he wasn't taking me seriously. Maybe he was right. After all, he *was* the police inspector.

Chapter 8

When we alighted from the train in Kampala, we might have been any couple on safari. Our disguise was assured when we were met by a tall thin African with ebony skin, wearing khaki shorts and shirt and desert boots. A pair of binoculars hung around his neck, and a water bottle in the case was attached to his belt on the right side.

He bowed slightly. "Welcome to Uganda, Juana, *memsahib*. I'm Joseph, and I'll be your driver and guide." He bent and picked up Ian's knapsack and my bag and started walking.

He led us to a minibus with black lettering on the side that said "Safaris, LTD., Kampala, Uganda," opened the door and helped us in. On the seat lay two hats: an Australian-type, digger hat with the brim turned back on the side; and a floppy, beige cloth hat with cords to tie under the chin.

Ian picked them up and burst out laughing. "You're almost overdoing it, Joseph," he said. "These hats are almost over the top, but we'll wear them anyway. Where did you get the minibus?"

Joseph slammed the door of the vehicle and took his place behind the wheel. He turned back slightly to talk to us.

"We had an old white minivan that some settler sold cheap when the family left the country. We kept it for when we wanted to do some inconspicuous surveillance. We thought about painting it in a zebra pattern, but it took us all night just to do the tan, and the lettering is barely dry."

"The binoculars are a good touch," Ian said. "They'll come in handy for whatever we might need to get a close look at."

"I have sharp eyes, Juana. I can find you the big game." He turned back and started the engine. The vehicle quivered as he turned out of the parking space, and I hoped it would get us there and back safely.

"To the Imperial Hotel," Ian said. "And I'll need you to wait."

"I am also a good shot," said Joseph, "and I brought along a rifle, in case we run into any dangerous game. In the back is your rifle, *Bwana*, and I procured a hunting license for you."

"You've thought of everything, Joseph. I can see why you were recommended for us.

At the hotel, Joseph opened the door and helped us out in a courtly manner and nodded when Ian told him to wait. He set down the knapsack and my pathetic-looking bag, and the barefoot bellman in a long white Kanzu came to fetch the bags and followed us to the reception desk.

"Mr. and Mrs. Alan Warner," Ian said.

The bellman snatched up the large key with the wooden tag attached, and loped off down the corridor. *I must now remember to think of him as Alan*, I thought.

"That's a good average name," I said in a low voice, as we followed the bellman.

"I thought about Albert and Elizabeth Windsor," Ian said with a smile. "But I thought that was a little obvious. Warner is not exactly a memorable name."

By the time we reached our room, the last on the corridor, the door was flung wide open and the bellman had already set the knapsack and bags on a luggage rack. I stared in dismay at the big bed, made up with an elegant taffeta coverlet, above which hung the usual mosquito netting, knotted up during the daytime. Without being asked, we had been assigned a bed meant for couples, not to singles, possibly because I was still wearing the wedding ring that Phillip had placed on my hand. *At least it might prevent a few people from thinking of me as Ian's popsy—or, as Allen's,* I corrected myself.

Ian handed the bellman two shillings, and the man said, "*Assante Sana,*" and left us.

"I have to nip down to the police headquarters and check over the details of what we'll be doing in the next few days. It looks as if Joseph has taken care of everything, but it always pays to double check and make sure. I'll be back as soon as possible."

I glanced at the bed, and, as if reading my mind, Ian said, "I'll stay on my side, if you stay on yours. I think you'll find everything you need in the bathroom, if you want to freshen up. Be sure to lock the door, or some cleaner may come in with no more announcement than a knock."

I nodded. "It won't take me but a moment to unpack. Shall I unpack for you as well?"

He laughed and said, "Acting like the good little wife, eh?" Then he left.

The room was dark and stuffy. I pulled aside the heavy drapes and opened the casement window to let in fresh air. It was barred for security.

I waited for what I thought would be enough time for Ian to get into the safari vehicle and leave, then I grabbed up my purse, took out the map and headed downhill to what I hoped was Franco's house. It was a short distance. I had the feeling someone was following me, but when I looked back, I saw only a figure bent over a rose bush in the hotel garden and an African digging in a flower bed with a *panga*. It was a

41

short, pleasant walk, and I enjoyed the heady fragrance of the evergreen hedge and eucalyptus.

When I knocked on the door, a servant opened it and let me in. I heard a voice call out, "Who is it?" A wiry little man who reminded me of Peter Lorie came toward the lounge.

On the coffee table I saw a cigarette lighter that I had seen Marcello use. *So, he has been here.* I picked it up and dropped it in my shoulder bag just as the man entered. "I am looking for Marcello. He gave me your address," I said, pointing to the map.

"Oh, you must be Joanna. He talked about you," he said, obviously expecting someone else. "Where *is* Marcello?"

"That's what I came to ask *you*," I said. "I know he's been here." I held out the cigarette lighter that I had pocketed. "This is his."

He had the grace to look embarrassed, and stopped trying to lie to me. "He came several days ago, but he didn't tell me where he was going, only to say that he had a job to do, and that when it was done he would take me out to dinner on his return."

He laid his hand on my arm, a hand that was cold, in spite of the tropical heat outside, and his eyes had a look that was almost of fear. "You're a nice woman, Joanna, better than Marcello deserves. Go home, and don't get involved in this. If Marcello had wanted you to know where he is and what he's caught up in, he would have told you."

He took the map from me and tore off the portion that contained his name and address. "I don't want anyone else coming here looking for Mar-*cello*."

"I'm already involved. I know what the plan is. They want to—"

"Stop!" he said, placing his hand on my arm. " Don't say a word about this. You never know who may be listening. The very servants and now households may be a part of it, or

42

they may turn us in. The less you know, the safer you are. Later, when it's all over, if Marcello comes back to you safely, you can sort things out and decide what you want to do about him."

"If he comes back?"

"Marcello is not always the man who sings to you and brings you gifts. He has a dark side. I hope you never have to see it."

"What do you mean?" I wanted to know more, and yet I didn't. I almost regretted coming to Franco's.

He dropped his hand from my arm and shrugged. "We grew up together, and I know the good and bad about him, and I accept him as he is, but I've seen how he can charm women. But I've said enough. You have to make up your own mind." He opened the door, and I knew he would say no more. He added only two words as I stepped outside: "Good luck." Then, as I started back up the hill toward the hotel, I saw him cross himself, just as he closed the door behind me.

Chapter 9

As I approached the hotel, I thought I saw movement within our room. Ian must have come back ahead of me. He'd want to know where I had been, and I wasn't sure how much I wanted to tell him. As was the custom, I'd turned in the room key at the desk when I went out, and when I entered the lobby, I looked up to the slot for our room, and saw that the key was missing.

The door was unlocked, and as I went in, I called out, Alan!"

There was no answer, and I heard a noise in the bathroom. I closed the door and would have locked it, but I didn't see the key.

The bathroom door opened, and a woman stepped out, pointing a pistol right at me. It was the woman from the train.

"What are you doing here in our room?" I demanded.

"Waiting for you to answer a few questions. Why are you in Uganda?"

"Going on safari."

"You don't expect me to believe that, do you? We saw each other in the morgue and I saw the coffin with Marcello's name on it."

"What I do is my own business, and how did you get in here anyway?"

"I gave the shamble boy a shilling, said I'd like to see what one of those rooms looked like inside, and asked what number this was. Then, all I had to do was ask at reception for the key in the slot for your number. Easy as could be."

I slid my hand toward the top of my shoulder bag. She had let the pistol droop a bit as she talked, but now she pointed it firmly at my chest. "Take off your bag and drop it on the floor!" she commanded.

I took it off slowly, but instead of dropping it to the floor, I hurled it at her. It knocked the gun from her hand, but before I could get to the purse and get my own, she grabbed up hers from the floor. " If you do anything else like that, I'll shoot you. I saw you going to Franco's, and I could have shot you then, but I'll let you go — or, maybe I won't. Did Franco tell you where Marcello is?"

"Why don't you go and ask him yourself?"

"I did ask, and he said that if Marcello had wanted me to know, he would have told me."

"That's exactly what he said to me."

She glanced down at the scattered contents of my bag. "Where did you get that cigarette lighter?"

"At Franco's house. I recognized it."

"I gave it to him," she said, surprising me.

"What is Marcello to you?"

"I had his baby when he worked here in Uganda. He promised he'd marry me, but then your husband died and you went after Marcello and took him away from me."

I saw the door opening slowly, and then Ian called out, "Josie! You forgot to lock the door."

As he burst in, the woman turned, startled, and I rushed at her, knocking her to the floor. The pistol flew out of her hand for the second time, and this time, I grabbed it, just as Ian grabbed the woman and pulled her hands behind her.

I kept her pistol trained on her with my right hand, while I raked the contents of my bag back into it and hoisted it to my left shoulder. Ian had her kneel, with her back to him and her hands pulled up painfully toward her neck, while he undid a small radio from his belt and called Joseph to bring the vehicle around to the front door of the hotel.

I found the room key in the bathroom, and locked the door behind the three of us. As we headed toward the lobby, Ian said, "We're going out of here as a threesome headed out for drinks. I've let your arms go free, but Josie and I will each take one, and I must warn you that I know several places I could press unobtrusively that would have you gasping for breath or paralyze you. Once we get out of earshot of the hotel, of course, I'll feel free to use the pistol." His voice was as even as if he were having a friendly chat with someone at the club.

We paused as I laid the key on the reception desk. "We're just going out to have tea," I said. " Only be gone for an hour or so. Should we just carry it with us?" I didn't want to say that someone had managed to get into our room by claiming our key. Ian could complain later about the lax security.

The clerk nodded and I dropped the key into my purse, hearing the metal key clank against the pistol I still carried. As we crossed the lobby toward the door, Ian said, in a very carrying voice, "It's been lovely to see you again. The next time we are back in town, we'll try to spend a longer time with you."

Joseph was well trained, and an excellent actor. He asked no questions about who his third passenger was and why she had joined us. As we drove away, the woman asked, Where are you taking me?"

"To the police station, of course," Ian answered. "We'll book you for entering premises without permission, taking a hostage, and — oh, yes — have time to check the pistol and see whom it's registered to."

The woman whimpered, "I wouldn't have killed you."

"You *did* threaten to. I stood outside and listened until I thought I had better break up your little twosome."

"What about her baby?" I asked.

"Joseph, can you have one of your fellows go around to her address and pick up the baby? We can find someone to take care of it as long as she's incarcerated."

"It died of malaria," the woman said.

If it ever existed, I thought.

As we drove, I studied her. Her black hair hung limp with perspiration, and her dark eyes smoldered with anger.

When we drew up and stopped in front of the white-painted police station and got down from the vehicle, I could almost feel the woman's mind working on her options. Could she escape and outrun us? Not likely. Could she grab one of the hunting rifles that were in the rear of the vehicle? No, they were out of her reach and bolted down, besides. Should she cry or apologize or perhaps flirt?

When we went inside, I knew for sure that flirting or crying would do her no good. At the desk that bore a sign that said "Chief Inspector O'Rourke," sat a beefy man with graying hair and the red skin that many fair-skinned Europeans acquire from time spent in the equatorial sun. The armpits of his tight khaki uniform were dark with perspiration, and a ceiling fan made a halfhearted attempt at cooling the room. Outside, the sky had grown dark and it looked as if rain was about to fall.

Chief inspector O'Rourke leaned back in his chair, which squeaked with his movement. "You were just here," he said, addressing Ian. "To what do I owe the honor of the second visit? And who are these women?"

"This is my wife, Josie. I registered for us both that we are in the country on Safari. This other woman—"

"That's not who she is!" the woman declared, cutting into Ian's statement.

O'Rourke turned on her savagely. "Silence! You'll have your chance to talk as soon as he finishes. If you interrupt again, I'll add time to your sentence."

And she bit her lower lip.

Ian continued. "This woman used bribery and fraud to gain entrance to our hotel room at the Imperial while my wife and I were out. When I returned, my wife was being held at gunpoint, and I overheard her being threatened. Her purse had been demanded, and its contents were scattered on the floor." (He said "my wife" in an easy manner, as if it were true.) "I subdued the suspect and took away her gun, while my wife gathered up the contents of her purse, including her own registered pistol. We escorted the suspect from the hotel and had our guide pick us up and bring us here."

While Ian talked, O'Rourke looked from him to me to the woman and back. He ran his hand through his hair and sat up straighter, looking at the woman. "All right, ma'am, it's your turn to talk. First, your name."

"This is all a misunderstanding," the woman said, leaning over toward O'Rourke and smiling. "I'm Fiona Jolley"

"You have a slight accent, which is not Scots as your name suggests. You look familiar. Where do you work?"

"I'm the bookkeeper at Singh Motors."

O'Rourke's eyes narrowed and he leaned forward on his desk, his arms crossed. "I knew you looked familiar. That's where I've seen you. Your Italian, and your name is Maria something."

"Ferretti," she admitted. "The manager can vouch for me."

"Vouch for what?" asked O'Rourke. His voice was louder, his words clipped. If he'd been a bull in the ring, he'd have had been snorting and pawing the dirt. "I'm charging you with unlawful entry, use of a weapon in a public building, and taking someone hostage. We'll check out that pistol of yours as well, and see which name it's registered to." He brought his hand down smartly on the desk and a sturdy black woman in police uniform came in.

"Matron, take this woman to the cell we have for women, and fetch her a change of clothing. She'll be with us for a week, possibly more."

Maria, as I now knew her to be, seemed to wilt and sag right before our eyes, and her skin looked so pale and bloodless that I thought for a moment she might faint. She opened her mouth to speak, then closed it and let herself be led away.

"Thanks, Paddy," Ian said. "I don't know what her game is, or which side she's playing on, but you have a week to find out."

O'Rourke had been watching the retreating woman, and now brought his attention back to Ian. "Glad to be of service, Chief Inspector Warner. If you have any more of her ilk, bring them to me. I wonder if we could get evidence of prostitution on her."

"I think you're charging her with enough."

O'Rourke rose, the two men saluted, and then slapped each other on the back. As we said goodbye, Ian said, "When we come back through, I'll buy you a drink, or maybe even a bottle."

"Always welcome," O'Rourke said. I wasn't sure whether he meant the bottle of whiskey or that we were welcome, and it didn't matter."

As we left the police station, rain suddenly poured down. We ran for the safari van.

Just those few steps in the rain were enough to drench me. My hair hung in untidy tendrils, with rainwater dripping off the ends of my hair, landing on my shoulders. Even though the temperature was warm, being wet made me feel chilled. Rain beat on the metal roof of the minivan, drowning out any chance of a conversation, and I had a head full of questions to ask Ian.

Joseph drove carefully, as the wipers swung back and forth across the windscreen. On both sides of the steep street, rivulets ran down beside the tarmac, red with mud from the loose earth, carrying bits of gravel, and where there was a drop in elevation, a miniature cascade dug out a gully below.

"This will spoil any chance of pretending we're on Safari," I said. "No one would be fooled into thinking we are taking a safari in weather like this. The animals will be hidden, and even if we saw any, we couldn't stand up and look out the sunroof."

"It won't spoil anything," Ian said quietly.

I turned to him in astonishment. "Isn't this the beginning of the long rains? How long will this last?"

"About two hours, I should say," he answered. "This isn't like Kenya. It rains like this nearly every day, from noon to two o'clock or so. We're on the equator and beside Lake Victoria.

"After a while, the rain will stop as suddenly as it began, and the sun will come out, and the earth will be all steamy, as the moisture gets sucked up into the air, ready for the next day's rain."

Joseph dropped us off under the portico of the hotel, and, as we got out, he reached into the back of the van and handed Ian a small leather suitcase, so shiny with newness that I looked for a price tag on it. When we got into our room, Ian tossed the suitcase onto the bed, unlatched it, and threw it open.

Chapter 10

"Dearest, I ordered these as a surprise for you, so you'll look like a safari lady should," he said, touching his finger to his lips to stop me from saying anything, and handing me a pair of khaki slacks and a matching bush jacket.

"Try these on. They'll at least get you into something dry. Let me see how you look, and whether Patel got a good fit."

"I'm beginning to dry off, just like the earth," I said, taking the garments from him. Mystified at the need for silence, I went along with his charade.

In the bathroom, I stripped off my damp clothing and pulled on the slacks. So far, so good. The bush jacket was a bit too large, but a cloth belt came with it.

When I came out of the bathroom and turned for Ian's inspection, he laughed. "A bit loose at the top, I'd say. Patel must think all American women have big bosoms. It will do, or shall we nip down and see if we can get it altered or exchanged?"

"I think it's just fine," I said.

"Good. Now, how about a quick lunch?" Ian glanced at his watch. "I think we can just about make it here before lunch time closes. By the time we finish eating, the rain will have ended."

"Yes, let's, Alan," I said, continuing to use our chosen names. "I'm starving."

We had chicken curry with all the condiments: chutney, peanuts, coconut, and chopped tomatoes. We finished with a cooling pineapple sorbet. Our table had a good view of the hotel gardens, and by the time we finished eating, I saw that Ian had been right. The sun was out and raindrops sparkled on small plants and glistened on the long fronds of shrubs. He took my hand to go out into the garden, and for a few moments at least, I felt as if we were really what we pretended, a young couple on safari.

As soon as we were out of earshot of any late diners, Ian said, "Walk slowly so you won't brush against wet plants, but every so often, bend to admire a rose or some other blossom. Smile as much as you can, as if you are enjoying our stroll. You must have some questions."

"Lots of them," I said, touching the wet petals of a deep red rose and pretending I was describing it to him. "First, why did inspector O'Rourke change his manner when he discovered that the woman's name was Ferretti?"

He laughed. "Because she's Italian. Paddy's never met an Italian he didn't dislike. It goes back to the Second World War. He was posted out here and assigned to manage the Italian prisoners of war. He was frustrated that they didn't understand English, and of course, they couldn't follow his instructions, but in spite of it all, they built a damned good road from here to Nairobi, up and over the escarpment."

We walked on to another rosebush, this one full of yellow roses, where we again paused. "I didn't like thinking about it. That's where Phillip's car went over the side and down to his death." I tried to keep a smile on my face, but it wasn't easy

"I'm sorry," said Ian. "I should have thought before I mentioned the escarpment. That wasn't all. Paddy was planning to marry a young Irish girl, and nurse, who was on her way to a hospital in Cairo when her ship was torpedoed. Paddy blamed the Italians for that — and, correctly."

I didn't know what to say. I felt sorry for his loss, and I understood it. "So, he's never married?"

"No. The Italians accepted being prisoners of war better than Paddy accepted being their guard. A great lot of them stayed on and sent for their wives and girlfriends, and are raising families here. So they're all around him. He's only got another year here, though, as independence comes and he's due for retirement about the same time."

We walked for a few moments in silence, turned left and walked past beds of blooming annuals. "Finally," he said, "Now it's my turn. First, I want apologize. I admit that I was dubious about what you said about Ms. Ferretti. You were right. I should have checked with police in Nakuru as soon as we got here. The package you saw must have contained the pistol. You were very observant and right to be suspicious. She could have killed you. Thank God I came back in time."

I straightened and smiled at him. "Thank you for that."

"Did Ms. Ferretti say anything of significance while she was holding you hostage?"

"She knows generally what Marcello is involved in, but she doesn't know where he is. She thought I knew."

Out of the corner of my eye I saw an African gardener come to a nearby flower bed, auger in hand, and squat to begin the work he had left off when the rain began. I was now suspicious of everyone around us. Anyone might be a spy.

"Pretend that I have told you some good news, and smile as we continue walking," said Ian. "Let's sit on that bench in the shade," he said, pointing. He led the way, and took out a large handkerchief to wipe the moisture off the bench before we sat down.

"Why do you think she was in Nairobi?" I asked.

He shrugged. "No way to tell until Paddy has had a chance to question her. I'll send him a message to ask her about that trip. Paddy would love to have a reason to grill her, and he's good at it. He's like the old Chinese water torture, without the water, or like a terrier that grabs hold of his enemy's leg and just won't let go. And since he soon has to return to the UK, this international case could be the crowning moment of his career, something that might even get him a bonus, but certainly a lot of praise from the higher ups. From my point of view, the main possibility is that she was escorting the casket to make sure it got to Nairobi intact."

"Could be either," I countered. "But I'm betting on intentional. Let's assume I'm right. She would have had an uneasy trip from Kampala to Nairobi, having seen Marcello's name on the coffin but not knowing if his was the corpse inside. At the morgue, she may have demanded that it be opened, and found as we did that it was some poor African. She knew, as we realized, that Marcello had been double crossed. She probably set out for Marcello's house to warn him, but of course, as you discovered, he was not there."

"Could she have beaten Kilonzo almost to death?"

"I doubt it. She probably had someone with her who had no qualms about beating an innocent African for information that he did not have."

"So he probably told them what he told me, the phone number he'd heard Marcello use. For them, it was a dead end, because they already knew about what was at the morgue. For you, it was a trail to follow. I think the morgue manager told her about your visit to Marcello's house

While we talked, the hot sun had dried all things to the point that I could hardly believe there had been a rain.

"By the way, I have further information about Kilonzo. He might lose the sight in one eye, and a couple of his crushed fingers may have to be amputated. We might be able to arrange some disability payments for him, in return for his helping the police in this smuggling case. I doubt if your

Marcello has made any provisions for health coverage or retirement. Few Europeans do."

"Why do you call him *my* Marcello?"

"You must care for him, or you wouldn't have put yourself in harms way as you have. So what is he to you? Or are you going to tell me it's none of my business?"

Chapter 11

"How well do you know Peter and Muriel?"

Ian responded, " I just have a brief acquaintance with them." He laughed. "Especially in Kenya, but all over East Africa, all the Europeans know each other—police, army, civil servants—everybody except you teachers get moved around all the time, like pieces on a chessboard. I met Paddy at Maralal when I first came out from the UK. He sponsored me for membership at the club, although it wasn't really necessary. We met again at Nan Yuki, where I was sent on a special assignment, and now we're working together, with me in Nairobi and Paddy in Kampala. East Africa is big in geography, but it's a small world socially."

"I'm still not sure how Ms. Ferretti knew the details about our journey. She rushed in out of breath, just as the train was leaving."

"And whoever was procuring a pistol for her didn't make it in time," Ian concluded. "My guess is, he hopped in his car and drove to Nakuru just ahead of the train, since he didn't have to make any stops, and that's where you saw him passing the gun to her."

Ian stood and reached for my hand. "Let's walk a bit more. Now, tell me how you know Franco, and what he said." He tucked my hand in the crook of his arm and pressed it close to his body, as if we were the loving husband and wife we pretended to be

I said, "I knew of him only because of what Marcello wrote on the map. Marcello has been to see him. Franco knows about the scheme, and he is scared."

Ian bent down as if he were about to whisper something romantic in my ear, but instead he said, "So I will have Paddy pick up Franco. What do you really know about Marcello?"

"I am not sure now. Some of the things that Franco told me made me think that Marcello might be living a double life, but to me he has always been a perfect gentleman. And he helped me through the worst of my grief over Phillip's death."

Ian snorted. "And well he should, since he *caused* Phillip's death."

"And that is what I need to know," I said. "That's why I am here."

He turned to me so that we were facing each other. "Now that you know how far-reaching this is and how dangerous, would you like to quit here and go home? I can arrange an escort for you."

I shook my head. "No."

"Because of Marcello?"

"No. Because of Kilonzo. He didn't deserve what happened to him. He wasn't involved. All he knew was that phone number, and it almost got him killed."

Ian looked surprised and asked, "Why did you go to Marcello's house?"

"The last time I saw Marcello, he told me he was going away on a business venture that was going to make him rich. He asked me to check his house while he was gone, and if he was gone too long, I was to contact Franco and someone else I have yet to meet. He wrote their information on the map that I showed you. Marcello was sometimes overly dramatic, and I was busy with end of term at school, and then I decided I should check up on Kilonzo in the house. After all, I had promised. When I found Kilonzo, I knew this was no robbery. Marcello had very few belongings. I think I would have reported it to the police, if you hadn't found me first."

"I'm glad you're going along, and Joseph and I will do our best to protect you. I don't think I would have made this trip by myself. Are you in love with Marcello?"

I didn't need to pause to think it over. I shook my head. "No, he was just someone to go out to dinner with. He's the cause of Phillip's death but we can't prove it. But I know in my gut that he did it."

Ian opened the door to the hotel lobby and, as I walked in ahead of him, he put his arm around me and said, "I'm glad you're staying, Josie. Right now, we need to dress for dinner."

OKAY, I KNEW FROM HAVING seen Ian the night before, how smashing he looked when he was dressed for dinner, and I was glad that Muriel had packed the emerald green cocktail dress for me. I didn't want to look at him, but I could feel his gaze on me. The dress slid easily over my shoulders and dropped smoothly into place. I reached back to zip it up, but he stepped forward and said, "Let me help you with that." I lifted my hair with my hand so it wouldn't get caught in the zipper. My bare skin tingled where he touched me. I could feel his breath warm on my neck as he zipped my dress. I wanted to turn into the warmth of his arms, but instead I stepped away from him. "Thank you," I whispered. "That was smoothly done. You must have had a lot of experience in zipping up women's dresses."

"I have sisters," he said.

He reached back on the bed and handed me a lightweight packet. "I took the liberty of adding this to our purchases this afternoon at Kerr Molly's. I think it's the kind of thing an upcountry wife or a tourist would buy."

I opened the packet and took out a shimmering, white silk stole shot through with gold threads. I wrapped it around my shoulders, tied loosely so that one end hung across my bosom. I needed some jewelry, but that was expecting too much of him. I had gold studs in my ears, and still wore my wedding band and the purple Tanzanian stone ring Phillip had given me. I turned before the mirror, and then back to face Ian. "It's lovely. Thank you.   I hesitated, then remembering, I said, "Alan, you seem to have thought of everything."

"You look lovely," said Ian. "I would like to take you out to dinner in Nairobi on a real date, not a pretend one like tonight."

"Hmmm. I'll say yes to an evening together," I said, "but perhaps I should be inviting you to dinner at the farm. I'm in debt to you for the clothing, and for providing the transportation to look for Marcello."

When Ian had been standing next to me, he was so close that I could feel his body heat, but at the mention of Marcello's name, he stepped back from me and his smile faded.

"I accept—unless Marcello is there. I doubt that will happen, if we are at all successful in the next few days, I want to see him in jail."

I didn't answer. Ian kept mentioning arresting Marcello, Franco had given me some warnings about him, and I knew that Muriel and Peter didn't like him, but I needed to hear from Marcello's own lips the truth about what he had done.

"Well, let's be off," Ian said brusquely, picking up the room key.

As we left the room, I reached for my shoulder bag.

"Don't put it over your shoulder," he said. "It spoils the look. Joseph will take care of it while we're having dinner."

"But what if I need it?"

"I have mine," Ian said, touching his left side. "Right now, this is one of the safest places in Africa. Theft is a

62

problem, but attacks on tourists just don't happen. People like Paddy and Joseph are respected and obeyed, and of course there's the *Kabaka*. God knows what happens to him after we leave. He's the hereditary ruler of the Buganda, but the other tribes have their own chieftains, and they don't care for King Freddie."

"So you think there's trouble ahead?" I asked, hardly believing that this lively polyglot city, this prosperous country that was called the jewel of Africa, would see bloodshed, but his words made me uneasy. He continued as we walked toward the front door. "They are against us right now, but after a few years of jockeying for power, they will start fighting among themselves, and it won't be safe for pale-skinned people like us—nor for the losing tribes, either." He put his arm around me, as the doorman opened the front door for us.

I saw the safari vehicle, it's pale sides easily visible among the dark Mercedes sedans and the few Rovers. Joseph started the engine and pulled up before the door to pick us up. I'd been used to climbing into the van in slacks, and my straight skirt was like a wide band around my knees.

Ian noticed, and helped me up into the van, his hands strong on my waist. I slid across the seat, and he climbed in and sat beside me, his thigh against mine.

It was only a short distance before we pulled up in front of a busy restaurant. La Quinta.

Even if I had tried, I couldn't have been heard over the sounds of laughter and music that poured from the lively nightclub. It was packed with people of all three racial groups clapping their hands to a calypso beat. We were shown to a table that bore a little card with the word "Warner" written on it. Ian and Joseph had thought of everything.

When he ordered Chateaubriand, I exclaimed with what I thought would pass for a worried look, "Oh, Alan! Can we afford this?"

"Dearest, of course we can afford it. This is our vacation, and we'll probably never be this way again. I intend to enjoy every hour of our trip, and every morsel of this wonderful food."

The owner played her part too, coming to our table and squeezing in beside me as the band quit. "Mr. and Mrs. Warner, it's so good to see you. I've been looking forward to your arrival, and we need to chat. A friend of yours was through here a few days ago and described you so well I immediately recognized you. He was most charming to me, even offering to take me along on a business deal to the Congo." She patted her non-blonde hair, and said with a smile and a shake of her head, "I told him no. It might make me a lot of money, but it could've gotten me killed. I told him that once I'd gotten out of the Congo all in one piece, I had no yearning to go back."

"Oh, I didn't realize you had lived in the Congo," Ian said.

"Oh, yes!" She sighed and seemed to be staring into space, or backward into time. "I had a beautiful place in Kivu. I loved it there. Kivu is beautiful, and I had an elegant French restaurant. But when all the fighting began, I knew I had to get out. Kivu is dangerous now. If you go there, you must be very careful." She touched my hand with her warm plump one. "I withdrew what money I had in the bank, all of it in Belgian Francs—before the Congolese printed their own money, you understand—and bought a bus ticket here. Kampala has been good to me. People like my restaurant, and I have done well with all the extra money I have made, which I sent out of the country, converted into British pounds, so if I decide to take a vacation there, I can afford it." She laughed lightly.

"You left everything behind in your restaurant?" I asked.

She nodded. "If I had stayed and waited for a good sale, they probably would have taken it from me and killed me, besides. Money is good to have, especially enough to ensure one's escape, but life and safety are more important."

She rose from the table. "You may run across your friend in Kivu. I think he was headed that way. Whatever you do and wherever you go, come back safely, and I shall see that you have another delicious Chateaubriand."

I was eager to get away and discuss with Ian what she had said, but he seemed in no hurry.

"This is worth every shilling I paid for it," he said, looking at me across his plate as he held a bit of Chateaubriand on the fork, and I realized that he had picked up on all the information Lisa had given us.

Finally, when our plates were cleared away, he ordered coffee with brandy, and while we waited for it to be brewed and delivered, he held my hand and said, "Josie my dearest, do you think we still remember how to dance?"

"Let's give it a try," I said.

He was an excellent dancer, despite his height, and moved with the grace of a lion for the fast number, and then held me close when the band moved smoothly into a slow romantic piece. I was sorry when he said, "Let's have our coffee before it gets cold and then say good night to Lisa. We have a big day tomorrow and a long way to go."

He told me to wait a moment at the table while he went back to tip Lisa. He tipped our waiter as well, and he knew and I knew that Lisa's was for information.

"I had Lisa call Joseph," Ian said, "and he'll be here shortly." As we walked to the door, Ian's arm around me, he whispered, "You seemed to enjoy yourself tonight."

"And why wouldn't I? Good food, good company, and a good dance partner. I'd like to have stayed longer."

"We have one more stop to make," he said. "And here comes Joseph."

Once again, he lifted me into the van, and, as we set off, he told Joseph, "Take us to Namirembe, the Cathedral."

"Why are we going to a Cathedral?" I asked. "We're not going to church tonight, are we?"

He laughed. "No, it's for the view."

As we left the downtown area, the streetlights—some of them in orangey yellow and others a bluish tint—became fewer and farther between, until the van was going up a hill in darkness. At the top, Joseph swung the van around so that we were pointed back toward town, and once again, I was assisted from the van onto solid ground.

"You can enjoy the view best outside of the vehicle," said Joseph. He doused the headlights on the van, and Ian and I stood looking down on Kampala. The lights below looked no larger than fireflies, and above us a thin bracelet of cloud slid across the moon. Any sign of rain had disappeared, leaving only that bit of cloud as a reminder. A hint of charcoal smoke hung in the air, and I could hear far-off drums—not death drums, but happy drums.

Then Ian put his arms around me and drew me close to him, bending down to give me a soft sweet kiss. As we drew apart, I said, "You're a good kisser, Mr. Warner, but we don't have to keep on pretending now."

"I'm not pretending," he said, leading me back to the van.

On the way back to the hotel, we felt free to discuss our trip the next day with Joseph.

"What did you get from my time with Lisa?" Ian asked me.

"That Marcello was here — that would be the friend she mentioned. I think he offered her a chance to get into the smuggling business with him or to perhaps be the point person here, which might mean he wants to get rid of Miss Ferretti. She told us to go to Kivu province in the Congo."

"But not to a specific location, unfortunately," Ian said. "And she warned us that it was dangerous."

"We already knew that," I objected. "And she said she brought out her money in Belgian Francs."

"That would have been the currency until lately, and that's the currency we found in the casket headed for Cairo, so that was nothing new," Ian concluded. "All in all, I'd say our evening was well spent."

"And so do I," I said.

Back in our hotel room, I saw that our room attendant had untied the mosquito net from its overhead knot, and it was now tucked in all around the mattress of our bed. The coverlet had been turned back invitingly, exposing plump pillows. An extra blanket was draped over a chest at the foot of the bed. Newcomers might laugh at the idea of a spare blanket in the tropics, but I knew that nights could get quite cool.

I was first to the bathroom, while Ian locked our door and windows, checking to make certain that all the locks were secure. He looked openly at me as I lifted the edge of the mosquito net and slipped in on my side of the bed.

When he came back, I pretended to be asleep, but he wasn't fooled. He leaned across and kissed me on the cheek, before pulling up the covers on his side of the bed

His voice reminded me of Phillip, with the same English accent that showed they had gone to the same public schools.

He wasn't as romantic as Marcello, but he was considerate of my needs and my feelings, and I felt comfortable around him. But he'd slipped so easily into the role of Alan Warner, that I thought he might be just an excellent actor and that once we had found his quarry, he'd take me back to Kenya and drop me off at the farm. Or he might not even go along, just send me with the police escort.

"Good night," I said.

Good night, dear," he said, as he turned onto his side away from me. The words were scarcely out of his mouth before he was asleep, snoring lightly.

I felt safe. I had retrieved my gun along with my purse from Joseph's care, and it was in the drawer of the night stand, right beside the bed. But my thoughts were in turmoil. Would we find Marcello alive, or would he actually be a body in a casket headed out of the Congo?

Chapter 12

When I awoke, the bed beside me was empty, and before I could stop myself, I rolled over and buried my face in the other pillow, seeking the familiar scent of Phillip. But, of course, it wasn't there; Phillip was dead. This pillow had an entirely different smell. Phillip had always had the aroma of the earth, for he spent his days walking about the farm plucking and squeezing a coffee bean to test, or whipping out his pocket knife to cut off a stray branch on a plant that the workers had somehow overlooked, and sometimes his hair had a smell of dust from the red earth that the cattle and horses kicked up.

Ian's scent was fainter and consisted of aftershave and soap. As I lifted the mosquito net and stepped out of bed onto the cool hardwood floor, he stepped out of the bathroom, freshly shaved and perfectly groomed, as he always seemed to be.

"Good morning," Ian said cheerily. "I'll look the other way while you go into the bathroom and get dressed. And I'll be handy when our morning tea is delivered."

I half wished that I had put on the lacy satin negligee Muriel had packed. It would be nice to have our tea leisurely. But what was I thinking? What did I care? We could be leisurely over breakfast in the dining room, or be served out on the veranda. Or maybe he wanted to have an early start anyway. My plain nightgown was anything but enticing. My nightgown was a serviceable garment, flannel. At least it didn't reveal my body beneath. I gathered up my clean underwear and my safari outfit, and made my way to the bathroom.

When I came out, the inescapable tea had arrived. That was one of the first things that I had discovered when I first arrived in East Africa. If one were staying at a hotel, someone would come and knock on the door in the early morning, and there would be a waiter or someone's servant bearing the tray of the morning tea.

Ian was sipping his tea and scanning the *Uganda Argus*, which had been delivered along with the tea. I sat down opposite him at the small roundtable, and accepted the cup of tea he passed across to me. "No real news," he announced, folding the paper and laying it aside. "Are you a morning talker, or do you need your coffee before you're fully alert?"

"The latter."

"So am I," he said. "Actually, I wake up alert, a habit military men and police either have or develop, however I *have* acquired a taste for your American coffee."

"I wake up fully alert, too—as well as early. I grew up on a farm, and a lot of work has to be done early in the morning. Then, out here, school always starts at seven-thirty in the morning. Thus, I am ready, or at least I will try to fit into your schedule." I nibbled on one of the biscuits, which turned out to be lemon flavored, and set my cup down.

Ian glanced at his watch. "Fine. The dining room should just be opening now, so probably we will be the first at breakfast."

He was right. When the waiter started to lead us to a table, Ian said, "Outside, please. We like to enjoy the fresh morning air." His hand was on the small of my back, urging me forward gently toward the veranda, and the commanding tone of his voice left no question as to what he wanted.

When we were seated, had given our orders, and a big pot of coffee along with the sugar and hot milk had been brought to our table, he said, "Now we can talk without being overheard."

I glanced around, seeing no other diners. The sun was just up and air was cool and fresh, and a crested crane, with its feathers fanned out majestically, strolled just outside the veranda wall. This was an East African morning at its best, and I wished that it might go on for a long, long time. But I knew that it wouldn't. I could push aside thoughts of why I was here for only so long, pretending that I was just having breakfast with someone I liked.

Ian seemed to feel that same way I did. He sipped his coffee thoughtfully, smiled, and said, "This is nice, isn't it, Josie?"

"Yes, it is, Alan" I said, playing my part.

He seemed as reluctant as I was to break the spell and face the reality of why we were here together. Our breakfast arrived: thick bacon; omelets folded and their ends cut off and discarded to form a perfect rectangle; triangles of toasts and tiny balls of butter resting on a plate.

"The first breakfast I have when I get home is going to be thin, crisp bacon, perfectly scrambled eggs, and either a hot biscuit with butter melted, or a stack of pancakes with maple syrup," I announced.

"May I be invited to your breakfast when you get home?"

"I mean in America, but you're invited if you're there."

He laughed. "It's a good thing no one is listening, or that exchange would have given us away." He signaled the waiter to take away our plates, poured us each more coffee, and I could tell he was now ready to talk. "There's no word from Paddy about Marcello's girlfriend," he said.

"Are you sure she's his girlfriend and not just his partner in crime?" I asked.

"Does it matter?" he asked, studying me.

I considered. "I don't know how I feel about him anymore.

"I've arranged for the police fund to take care of what medical expenses Kilonzo may have. I put him down as an informer."

After a moment, Ian pushed his cup aside and said, "We have been skirting around the past and future of Marcello. Let's face facts. Marcello may already be dead, but if he is alive we have got to arrest him and charge him, not just with smuggling, but with Phillip's murder."

"Phillip wasn't murdered. He died in an automobile accident," I objected.

Ian shook his head slowly, and made a sound. "You Americans," he said. "There's no such thing as an automobile accident. Things don't happen by accident. There's always a cause and often several causes that come together. The correct term is car crash. Your Phillip died in a car crash and it was caused by Marcello."

"How can you say that? Marcello wasn't with Phillip when he went off the road and down the escarpment."

"He wasn't in the vehicle with your husband, but we think he was close behind. He was the one who flagged down a motorist to send for the police.

"Think back to the day of the accident. Who brought you the bad news?"

"It was Marcello," I admitted, recalling that sad afternoon. "He had gone to bring Peter and Muriel along, and he left soon afterward, and then the police arrived."

"Do you recall what he told you?" Ian asked.

I thought for a moment before I answered. "He told me he had bad news, and he thought I might want some company. He said that Phillip's car had gone over the escarpment, and the police were trying to get the car and him back onto the pavement. He didn't say Phillip was dead."

Ian took a sip of his coffee before he went on. "Did you wonder why he arrived there before the police? And why he knew what had happened?"

"No. I suppose I must have thought that he came upon the accident before anyone else noticed that a car had gone over the edge. I was grateful that he had thought to have Muriel and Peter come over to be with me. We were hoping for the best, of course." I closed my eyes, remembering that evening.

"After Marcello left, Muriel started to make some tea, but Peter intervened to pour me a glass of brandy. Muriel said she'd stay with me until we knew Peter was all right, and emphasized that I shouldn't be alone at such a time. Naturally, Peter offered to take me to Nairobi if Phillip were badly injured and needed to be hospitalized."

"And what exactly did the police tell you?" Ian asked, bringing me back to the present.

I tried to remember what had been said, but my mind was a blank. "I don't remember anything after he told me that Phillip was dead. I think I fainted. The next thing I knew, I was lying on the sofa with a light blanket over me, and Muriel was sitting in a chair beside me." (I felt tears begin to form, and I swallowed to keep from sobbing.) "Muriel took me to identify Peter's body, and to make funeral arrangements. When the policeman came to see me a few days after the funeral, he asked me if Phillip was a heavy drinker. I told him that we had wine when we went out to dinner, and a drink at the clubhouse, but when he was driving, he limited himself to one beer, even after a rugby match. The policeman said he had asked other members of the rugby team and they told him the same thing. Then, he asked me if Phillip was a good driver, and I said, of course he was. Again, he nodded and said that was consistent with what his teammates had said about him."

I picked up my coffee cup, but it was empty. I had a lump in my throat that threatened to choke me because of what I had to say next. I picked up the glass, took a drink of water, and waited until Ian signaled the waiter for fresh coffee before I went on. "Then he asked me if I thought Phillip was suicidal—as if my wonderful happy husband wanted to kill himself. I screamed at him to go away, and he picked up his cap and left. Why are you opening up all this again?"

Our coffee arrived, and Ian filled two cups and added the hot milk. My hands shook as I picked up the cup to drink.

"We police have to consider all the possibilities," Ian explained. "The inspector had ruled out poor driving, drunkenness, and an intentional crash. Didn't you wonder why your husband had run off the side of the mountain and died?"

"Of course. I agonized over it and told myself a hundred times that I should have gone along with him."

"Then you would also probably be dead at this moment," he said harshly. "There were no skid marks to indicate that Phillip had attempted to stop before going over, and he was a healthy young man who had just played a winning game, so there was no reason to suspect a heart attack or him falling asleep at the wheel. That left very few other possibilities, the obvious one mechanical failure. It was some time before we could get all the pieces of the car brought into our inspection garage. The brake line had been cut, and the bumper had been shoved into the rear of the car which is unlikely in a front-end crash or a rollover. Are you following me so far?"

I could only nod mutely, playing out in my mind, as I had so often, Phillip's last moments.

"Who do you know who's skilled at working on car engines, and who was very soon on the scene? And who just might have given Phillip's car a push with his own just as the two vehicles started down the escarpment? I come up with only one name, and that is Marcello. Didn't you think it was strange that at the last minute he called and asked Phillip to drive by himself, claiming that he needed to see a friend in Uganda? And then, after the game, he was not in Uganda, but was headed back to Nairobi, driving closely behind Phillip, so that he was the one who called for help after the crash."

"But why would he do such a thing?" I demanded, seeing that everything Ian said put suspicion on Marcello.

Ian stirred his coffee and then took a drink before he went on. "Phillip called our office from the White Stag using the phone in the cloak room. And he left a message to say he would come by my office on his way home to tell me something important. I wish he had said what it was or mentioned Marcello. That would have made our job much easier. "

When I didn't say anything for a moment, Ian went on. "We think during the rowdy drinking that followed, Marcello slipped out and cut the brake line. He was a good mechanic, and worked at the motor works before he got the job at the cement factory. He would know exactly what to do and how to do it quickly, and you probably know how rowdy those celebrations can be. No one would have missed him for a few minutes, or if they did, they'd assume he was in the loo."

"I still can't believe it. How could he be so cruel to a friend?"

"He probably wouldn't think of it as cruel, if he gave it a second thought at all. For him it was merely survival, getting rid of the snitch. We were prepared to arrest him immediately after the crash, but we decided instead to let him think he's gotten away with it, and had him followed. Nothing we do can bring Phillip back, and he was a fine man. But if we can break up the smuggling ring, we may save the lives of several others and stop an international crime ring."

Ian laid his hands on the table and leaned back, waiting. "So if he admits he killed Phillip, could you shoot him?"

"I don't know," I responded.

When Joseph arrived in the safari vehicle, I'm sure he noticed the stiffness between Ian and me. Body language can show more than mere words. He stowed our suitcase and helped me into the van, sliding the door closed after Ian, and taking his place behind the wheel. Only then did he turn back and ask a single question, "Are we ready to set off on our safari?"

When Ian nodded, Joseph started the engine and we left the Imperial hotel behind us.

NEITHER IAN NOR I HAD anything to say to each other as we maneuvered the clogged streets of Kampala and headed out. The morning mist was beginning to clear in the hot sunlight, and I studied the colorful panorama of an African road, concentrating on what I was seeing instead of thinking of Phillip or Marcello.

Joseph was a good driver, maneuvering around bicycles that wobbled into our path, often with a woman in a colorful dress sitting sidesaddle behind the cyclist, and even more often carrying cargoes of charcoal, bananas, or even electric appliances. When we had to stop for masses of people on their way to market or to church, children ran out calling, "*Baksheesh,*" with hands outstretched for money. In the city, I had seen Buganda women walking tall and proud in their typical attire—a brilliant colored dress with square neckline and big sleeves, fitted at the waist and then flowing to about knee length, with what appeared to be a skirt of the same fabric below, which reached to the ankles. These were prosperous women, and this attire was one of the symbols of their prosperity.

As we set off on our journey westward, I was troubled at all that Ian had told me. Why could I have been so fooled and beguiled by Marcello that I never suspected him of being involved in Phillip's death?

Ian's description of the evidence seemed compelling that Phillip's death had been no accident, and I recalled that, at the time of the funeral, Phillip's father kept saying, "I don't understand it, not at all." It was he who had in fact made a trip to Nairobi and demanded that the police launch a full investigation of the crash, not just writing it off as "accidental."

Phillip had grown up in Kenya and was used to all the roads, especially the one over the escarpment, and I had ridden with him on that route, going to rugby games.

Phillip's mother, between sobs, had said that we might as well let it go, as nothing could bring back Phillip, and that was the way I felt.

"I have to do this to get it straight in my mind," Phillip's father had said. "They'll pay attention to me, at least as long as the Brits are in charge, because I still carry some weight here and in the UK. Joanna, you might have the American Embassy look into it, although they might say it doesn't concern them, as Phillip was not an American."

I vowed that I would ask the embassy to use their clout to push for an investigation, and I would demand to see all the crash reports that the Kenya police had.

That is, if we got out of this alive.

Chapter 13

Even if Marcello was not guilty of killing Phillip, but only of smuggling, I didn't think I wanted to have anything more to do with him. But this wasn't the time to decide. *I'll just enjoy the countryside.*

Outside the city, where there were no paved sidewalks but only dusty red earth, pounded bare and flat by tens of thousands of feet, the women wore much simpler dresses, straight and loose — perhaps introduced by missionaries.

Uganda was a prosperous country, and the Buganda province that we were passing through was the largest and most prosperous of the country. The Brits referred to it as "the Pearl of Africa." In my brief orientation before I began teaching in Kenya, I'd gone with my group on a field trip to see coffee and tea plantations as well as the sugar mill, the fabric mill, and the hydroelectric dam on the Nile River at Jinja. Now I was trying to think about those visits, instead of envisioning Phillip's mangled body and his car. The sugar mill was the most interesting, with the heady, almost overwhelming, aroma of sugar cane being ground, the juice cooking, and eventually becoming brown, granulated sugar — none of your sparkling white cubes — but sugar still the same, with some of the syrup still in it. The fabric mill had been so noisy that talk was impossible, as the huge machinery spun Uganda cotton into threads, and other machines rolled out great bolts of cotton fabric, which were then sent to be dyed.

The dam at Jinja was like all hydroelectric dams the world over: the backed-up water of Lake Victoria flowed through turbines and spewed out in foamy swirls below, from whence it would eventually find its way through the Sudan and Egypt and out to the Mediterranean.

I was jerked out of my reverie, when Joseph braked for a man running across the road right in front of us to catch a bus that was about to pull away; our safari van narrowly missed hitting him. He clambered onboard, joining the passengers, bicycles, and crates of animals. We followed the bus for perhaps a mile, choking in the blue smoke that issued from its exhaust, before Joseph was able to make his way around the lumbering vehicle, and, for a moment, we were on open highway.

Away from Kampala, the highway grew narrower, and there were fewer bicycles, but now we began to see herdsmen in loose brown garments that reminded me of pictures in an illustrated Bible storybook my mother had once bought me, driving herds of goats and occasional cattle. The women were wrapped in colorful lengths of bright, multicolored cloth referred to as "*Mericani*." Beside the road, coffee trees had white blossoms amid the red mature berries that were so like my own coffee farm back in Kenya, and in the far distance, I could see the faint outlines of mountains.

"We passed the first test out here," Ian said, breaking into my observations.

"What do you mean?"

"The children. Those little beggars took us for tourists. They never would have dared beg if we'd been in a police vehicle. Let's hope the adults take us for granted as well."

Joseph had kept the sun roof and the windows closed because of the dust, and the van had grown stuffy. He now opened both, and I enjoyed the cooler air as we climbed upward.

We passed women carrying huge earthen jugs of water on their heads. When I'd first seen them, I thought they must have flat top heads, but of course that was silly. Ian laughed when I told him about my early mistake. "They have little platforms woven of grass or sisal, that are flat on top and fit the curve of their heads below," he explained.

"Oh, I know that now."

Later, when the road had turned to dirt and we crossed the equator, with a big circle marking the spot, Joseph played the part of tour guide, and stopped so we could each take a picture of ourselves posing, standing within the circle, hands raised to touch the upper edge.

As we pulled away from the sign, a car drove by, and right behind it was a much better safari vehicle than ours — with viewing seats raised high in the wide open air. It bore the name of an international tour company, and the tourists sitting up on the back seat wore hats like something out of old movies: pith helmets with flaps hanging down. The tourists waved gaily and the four of them clambered out as soon as the vehicle pulled into the spot we had just vacated.

"Clearly tourists," Ian observed, and I laughed as we waved back at the group.

"Should we have gotten hats like those?" I asked.

"I don't know where they found those getups," Ian said. "They're almost *too* touristy. I think they would fool anyone who saw us."

He was right, and it almost cost us our lives.

We stopped again when we saw some children selling a huge bunch of bananas. Joseph got out and chatted with them for a moment, then came back bearing the bananas, as the children waved and smiled. The bananas were the small, sweet, thin-skinned kind called "finger bananas." They had a lot more flavor than the big commercial ones I was used to in America.

"How much?" Ian asked. "I'll have to put it on the expense account."

"Two shillings," Joseph said over his shoulder. "I didn't bargain very well."

"Two shillings?"

"What a bargain," I said.

"You're really talking like a tourist, *memsahib*," Joseph said. "I could have gotten that much for a shilling, but an extra shilling will make them happy, and if anyone comes looking for us and happens to ask these children, they'll remember the generous tour guide."

In a few moments, Joseph signaled and turned onto a narrower road, bordered on both sides by tall grass. Unlike Kenya, all of Uganda seemed well-watered, and the ground was actually a bit muddy.

"Where are we going?" I asked. "Is this the way to Kivu?"

Ian shook his head. "We're not going there. We don't need to."

"But Lisa said —"

"She told us where the treasury had been, not where it is now." He emphasized the two verbs.

"But why did she tell us so much about Kivu?"

"Self protection, probably. I have no doubt that she was correct about its early storage, but if she had kept that a secret, she might have been killed. By telling other people, especially the police, she's made sure she's not the only one who knows, just in case. Keeping it in the Congo would have been risky. The whole idea is to get it safely out of the Congo and out of Africa to some bank in Europe where people don't ask questions about who owns the fortunes that are brought to them. Keeping the treasury in Africa, especially in the

Congo, would require twenty-four-hour-a-day protection by a large force. Thieves know that they may be killed by other thieves. Hence, the coffins."

Joseph said in his best tour guide manner, "We are in Queen Elizabeth Park, one of the largest game parks in all of Africa, and as big as some of the smaller states in Europe." As he spoke, we came in sight of the small ranger station. A Rover, painted in jungle camouflage, was parked beside the small shed, its nose pointed out to the road. A ranger stepped out from the post, clipboard in hand, and Joseph hopped down from our vehicle and went to speak with the rangers and sign in for us.

When he got back into the safari van, he said, "They reported a good-sized herd of elephants. A few miles on, there are picnic tables. We can stop there for lunch."

"The bananas?" I asked.

Joseph shook his head. "No, *memsahib*. Your tour guide has packed sandwiches, cheese, and chocolates, as well as flasks of tea. It's in a hamper in the back, along with serviettes and the jug of water to pour over your hands before you eat."

"Bravo, Joseph!" Ian said.

Just then, the silvery, green grass parted and a huge elephant emerged, blocking our way. Joseph stepped on the brake, and we fishtailed to a stop no more than six feet from the magnificent creature. It towered over the van, its huge ears flapping slowly. It raised its trunk toward us, as if checking the air for some danger we might carry.

I sucked in my breath, awed by the site. I had never been so close to an elephant.

Ian handed the camera to Joseph, who began clicking away at the elephant.

"I've never seen such tusks," Ian said in a hushed voice. "I've never seen a pair quite like that. I can't even imagine how much they would bring on the Chinese market."

Joseph turned, handing back the camera. "That's what the rangers are trying to stop. Once these elephants are gone from Uganda, they'll never return. Some higher ups in the government are making a fortune selling tusks — selling their heritage and our future. Tourist don't come to East Africa for the food or the nightlife, they come to see the animals that God has put here for us."

"They're precious," Ian said, handing the camera to me. "You take this, and I'll keep the binoculars around my neck." Looking back at the elephant, he added, "Small creatures multiply fast, and have multiple babies. It takes an elephant twenty-four months to create a new one. A mother could have two human babies, or even twins or triplets in the time it takes an elephant to make just one. They're losing the race with people."

The elephant turned away from us and walked on, followed by three other elephants: one half-grown, and one a youngster that trotted valiantly to keep up.

"I'm so glad we saw them," I said. "Whatever else happens today, I'll think of this moment. Elephants are such wonderful animals, the best of all. They're better than humans. They don't commit crimes and they care for each other."

"Spoken like a true tourist," Joseph said, putting the van in gear and easing along the road, glancing from side to side in case there were other animals ready to enter the road.

True to the ranger's directions, we saw a red dirt pull-off area up ahead, with two wooden picnic tables in the shade of acacia trees. Recent rain had left the ground muddy, and the van bounced into and out of potholes. Joseph spread a checked tablecloth on one of the tables and set out our lunch.

It was suitably elegant to be a safari lunch. Joseph had even provided a small towel to dry our hands after we poured water over them.

Trees grew luxuriously around us, and off in the distance we could see Ruwenzori — the mountains of the moon. There was a slight breeze to cut the heat and humidity, and it carried a fragrance of something spicy and woodsy.

"I wish I could stay here all day," I said. "It's so pleasant."

"You can have all the picnics you want after we complete our mission," Ian said. Joseph was backing away with our picnic things in the van when a shot rang out. Ian stood, looking in the direction the shot had come from, and Joseph poked his head out of the van. "Was that what I think it was?" he asked. "It sounded close by."

"Go get in the van," Ian commanded me. "I'll take a look and see where it came from."

I swung my legs back up and over the seat of the picnic table, but before I could stand and run to the van, two men wearing camouflage pushed their way through the underbrush, one with a heavy duty rifle slung over his shoulder. His skin was tanned, but I could tell he was a European, as East Africans referred to anyone with white skin. His companion, a tall African with gleaming black skin, had a pistol, which he swung back and forth, pointing first at Ian and then at me.

Chapter 14

"Don't move!", the lighter-skinned man said, unslinging his rifle and also training it on us, or rather, on Ian. My mouth felt dry, and I had to lean against the rough wood of the seat to keep from collapsing. I'd been uneasy when Ms. Ferretti held a pistol on me, but mainly because her hand was so shaky, I didn't know just where she might aim. These men were different. They knew exactly where to aim, and while I didn't know why they were pointing weapons, or just where they had come from, I was paralyzed with fear.

"My favorite targets," the light-skinned man said. "You tourists are so careless. It almost takes the fun out of robbing you. But I won't let that stop me. Dump your valuables on the table—cameras, binoculars, watches, jewelry all of it. He looked toward the van. "You, black boy, get out of the van." His companion with the pistol started towards Joseph.

Instead, Joseph swung into the seat, started the engine and roared off, flinging mud all over everything.

The man with the rifle cursed, and then laughed. The black man laughed too, and started toward me. The rifleman turned to his partner. "Not now. We've got all the time in the world, at least until some car passes by. Just search them first."

I heard the *chug chug* of the bus making its way up the hill. Maybe they would help us! What if I ran out to waive, flagged it down? As it came into sight, I half rose and waved my hand.

"Sit down," said the rifleman. And if you scream, I'll kill you."

I sank down onto the rough wood, facing the road. At least if Ian and I had a chance to run, I wouldn't be trapped with my legs inside the picnic table. Why did all the picnic tables in the world have to be built that way ? But that was a foolish, useless question at this time.

No one on the bus paid any attention or seemed concerned. Well, a few did, after opening a window to look at us, but it was clear that they didn't want to have anything to do with our situation. And why would they? Our two captors wore camouflage, looking like game rangers, and game rangers carried guns. To them it must have seemed that rangers had caught us doing something illegal, or maybe they were just asking us questions about why we were there — and where our vehicle was.

Ian put a hand on my arm, and I didn't know if it was meant to comfort me, console me, or warn me. I had never been in a situation like this — helpless and terrified.

The bus paused for a moment, and I had a quick flash of hope that the driver might at least ask us if we needed help, but instead he put the bus into a lower gear to maneuver up the muddy hillside.

How I wished I had my pistol! I felt sure that if I had it, I would have tried to kill both our captors, and if Ian had had his pistol, he would have shot the rifleman, at least. But my pistol was in my shoulder bag, which was in the van, and Ian's was in the knapsack. We had tried to look like tourists on safari, and tourists wouldn't have been allowed to carry a weapon. We had succeeded too well.

Joseph, our game guide, would have been expected to carry a weapon, but he had abandoned us, driving away after being shot at. We were all prepared to face smugglers the next day, not criminals—probably poachers who had shot an elephant with that first shot we heard.

"No one's going to help you," the rifleman said with a laugh, "not even the man you paid to bring you here." He motioned to his companion with a slight swing of the rifle, and I felt Ian move beside me as the rifle swung back. "Don't try anything!" he barked. "Go ahead!"

I had nothing for Esau to find. I had already taken off my watch and laid it on the table beside our camera and the binoculars. That didn't stop Esau from running his hand into my trouser pocket and clutching my legs tightly as he did so, the gun in his other hand touching my neck. He brought his hand out and opened it to show a Kleenex tissue and two hard candies.

"That's it?" The gunman asked in disgust. "Take off your rings."

"No! All I have on is my wedding ring."

"It's gold. It will bring a few dollars. Take it off and hand it to Esau, or I'll have him chop off your finger."

I hadn't even noticed a *panga* hanging from Esau's belt. I knew that one stroke of the *panga* could cut my hand off. I pulled at the ring, my hand slippery with sweat, and managed to pull it off. It hit the table, bounced, and fell through the space between two of the table boards. Esau bent to look at it, but the rifleman cried, "Leave it! Get the man's wallet!"

The rifleman pointed his weapon at Ian's chest. "Get out, with your legs out from under the table, and stand up so I can see that you're not hiding anything, and it'll make it easier for Esau to search your pockets."

Ian did so, and this meant we both had our backs to the road, so we couldn't signal for help. The rifleman must have heard the sound of approaching vehicles, as I did. It sounded like a Rover.

Esau took Ian's wallet and handed it to the rifleman, who said, "Cover them, Esau, and don't be afraid to shoot." He flipped open the wallet with one hand, and read what I realized was Ian's fake identification. With his thumb and finger he opened the compartment where money was kept, and smiled with pleasure. "Oh, we found ourselves a rich one, Esau." He managed to deftly extract the money, letting the rifle droop for a moment as he put the money into his pocket, and flung the wallet on the table. It landed behind Ian.

"You've got all we had," Ian said. "What are you going to do with us now?"

"I thought about taking you along with us, but you would just be in the way. So I'll leave you here. Maybe some kind motorist will come along and help you. Maybe not. You don't have any money or even any food or water or any way to protect herself. You don't know my name, and I doubt if you could describe Esau well enough for the police or the game rangers to arrest him. So—"

Suddenly there was a great bellow, shaking the earth like thunder, as a huge bull elephant crashed through the bush. The rifleman turned to escape but it was too late. With one huge foot, the elephant knocked the man to the ground and stomped on his chest knocking the life out of him in seconds. With a second foot, the rifleman's face was crushed beyond all recognition. What had been an arrogant threatening man, an elephant killer, was now a mass of bloody, inert flesh.

Esau ran, as a second elephant emerged from the bush. It picked him up with it's trunk and flung him to the ground with a bone-breaking thud.

I watched, paralyzed. Would they come for Ian and me next? Ian was gripping my arm, pulling me behind him. The big bull elephant turned over the table spilling all that was laid on it.

The mighty bull waved his trunk in the air and emitted a bellow of satisfaction. He had avenged the killing of his elephant kinsman. Both elephants walked with great dignity into the bush just as our van and a Rover full of game rangers swerved into the pullout.

I stood, shocked, leaning against Ian and unable to speak.

Rangers scrambled out of the Rover, as Joseph climbed down from the van, all carrying rifles.

"What took you so long?" Ian asked, as calmly as if we'd been waiting on the street corner for friends who were late for dinner. "Another few minutes and both of us might have been shot."

"We got back here as quickly as we could, given the state of the roads," Joseph said. "You must have known I wouldn't abandon you."

Ian nodded. But we had to pretend that we thought so."

The ranger walked over to the fallen rifleman. "Looks like Milton," one of them said. "We've been on the lookout for him, and, so it seems, has the bull elephant. Makes me sick to my stomach to see dead elephants that he's killed." He bent for a closer look.

The second ranger turned him over. "He's dead. Elephants know what they're doing. His gun is bent out of shape as well."

"What were they doing here?" Ian asked.

"Either waiting for transport to come along, or their vehicle is up the road a bit, and they were planning on hitching a ride, with the robbery thrown in. You two did us a favor by keeping them occupied here until we arrived."

Joseph pointed at dark shapes in the sky. "Vultures have sighted the carcass."

The ranger stood up from Milton's body. "We'll have to take him to headquarters and arrange for someone to identify him. I'm about ninety percent sure he has no identification, or if he does, it's fake. His money is scattered all over the place here, though."

"That would be mine," Ian said, picking up his wallet and opening it to show its emptiness. The ranger handed the money he had picked up to Ian.

"Want to go for a hike down the hill and take a look at the mourners?" the second ranger asked. "It's a sight you'll never forget. The herd circles the body of their friend and stays for days, touching the dead one with their trunks, and crying as humans do."

"Elephants are better than some humans," Joseph said.

"They care for each other," said the first ranger. "They don't fight or steal, and they rear their young to grow up to be well-behaved. Elephants and pigs are two of the most intelligent of all animals, and if either had opposable thumbs, they'd give us a run for our money. They know when one of their own has been killed, and they even know when humans who have been kind to them die."

The other ranger said, "I wish every poaching would end as this one has. We do what we can, but we are fighting our own government leaders all over Africa. They buy the tusks from the poachers for a pittance and sell them in Asia for a fortune."

The other ranger took up the story. "Elephants have a keen sense of smell, and undoubtedly tracked Milton here. And they know how to get revenge when they need to. The only enemies they have are humans with high-powered rifles. In the end, they lose to what we call civilization."

I didn't want to see a dead elephant, although I would have liked to find some way to thank the big bull that had probably saved our lives.

Ian and Joseph had picked up the camera, binoculars, and our watches. I was about to tell them to forget about my wedding band, so that we could be on our way. I wanted to leave that terrible place behind. Then Ian held up the ring. "Here we are, dear," he said. "Hold out your hand."

I did, and he slipped the ring onto my finger, almost as if we were wedding each other. He closed my hand with his, and then said, "Let's be on our way. We still have a lot to do and a long way to go."

Emilee Hines

Chapter 15

Later, I had no memory of getting into the van, or of what scenery we passed for the first score of miles. My mind had shut out what had happened, just as if it had happened to someone else. When I was next aware, I was shaking with sobs, as tears poured down my face, and Ian was holding me against his chest, and rubbing my back gently.

"I'm sorry," I managed to say. I fumbled in the pocket of my slacks for a tissue, but Esau had taken everything from my pockets, so I just let the tears fall. I eased back slightly from Ian, but stayed close enough to feel the comforting warmth of his body. "You probably think I'm going to be a burden, crying all the time."

"No," he said. "What happened back there was pretty horrific."

"I've never seen anyone killed," I responded.

"It was ghastly, but it was quick," he said. Then, looking away, he added," The poacher may have had something painful in mind for us. I was planning to grab Esau's gun and kill Milton myself, but the elephant took care of that little matter for us."

"I hate him, hate him! I hate anybody who kills elephants. I'll remember to the end of my life the mournful sound that elephant made. And he cried real tears, just as a human being would."

"I hate him too," Ian said. "And I hate the buyers of elephant tusks. But I can't much blame an African who is paid more for one night of helping to track and kill an elephant than he would make in six months of working on the sisal or coffee plantation. I blame the Chinese, Thais, and other Asians, who get fantastic prices for little trinkets — jewelry and little carvings made out of the tusks. I blame them also for that absurd belief that drinking ground rhino horn makes them more . . ." he hesitated ". . . *masculine*. They must be very insecure if they think they even need an aphrodisiac."

At that, I laughed. I moved so that I could look at Ian's face. "You obviously don't feel any such need." After a pause, I asked the question I had wanted to ask from the first time I'd met him: "Are you married? I know there are men who come out to Africa to work, leaving their wives at home in the UK."

Ian responded, "I'm not one of them. Not married, divorced, widowed — *or* gay "

"Why haven't you married?" I asked. "You're certainly eligible."

It was his turn to laugh. "That's an old-fashioned word. "What makes me *eligible*, other than being a man?"

I hesitated and then went on, studying him, as if I were seeing him for the first time: the wavy blonde hair that seemed to never be out of place, even now after the days experience, blue eyes, perfect features, and a trim, muscular body. "You're intelligent, you have good table manners, and you know how to comfort a woman. I'm surprised some woman hasn't snapped you up."

"You've undoubtedly heard the saying, 'Are you married or do you live in Kenya?' There's a scarcity of women out here as you may have noticed, even in your American Teachers Project, and I seldom stayed put long enough to establish a relationship with a woman, even if they had been around. How much do you want to know?"

"As much as we have time for. After all, we're supposed to be married and on Safari. I want to know all kinds of things about you, in case we run across people you already know, or people who are nosy while trying to be friendly."

He nodded. "Very well, my life's story, and it might bore you, but after all, you started it. I attended what we Brits call a good public school, where of course there were no girls. I had a scholarship, as my father had been killed in the war, and my mother couldn't have afforded the school otherwise. I owed it to her to get good grades, so I hit the books. I also played sports, and I made some lasting friendships. Once in a while, one of the fellows would invite me to come home with him during holiday time, and he'd introduce me to his sister, but since I had no title or fortune, the girls were never interested in the long run. I was accepted to the London School of Economics and spent a year there before I was called up to do my National Service, but I think I told you about my life."

"Well, now I'll add to your list of good qualities that you are interesting. Were you ever frightened?"

"Not so much in Malaya, although we were dropped down behind the line and left to use our survival techniques. In Kenya, I led a group of Africans against other Africans, and I was bloody well scared. For one thing, I never knew which of my troops might be Mau Mau. They could have turned on me, but I couldn't let my fear show, and after a while my fear went away."

"And what are your requirements for a wife," I asked, "if you ever settle down long enough to find one?"

He shrugged and studied me much as I had studied him.

"Well, you *know* you're eligible. I'm sure you could have the pick of half the men in your teaching group, not to mention the single Brits who are out here, commissioners and

97

such. Besides being attractive, you own property, although some African politician may take it over after independence and give you a pittance for it."

"My, but your swelling my head," I said. "So, let's try it another way. When you do finally settle in one place long enough, what kind of woman are you looking for?"

"One who loves me," Ian said, surprising me. He had seemed so unemotional about things that I hadn't thought about him as romantic. "Nice-looking, but not beautiful," he went on. "Beautiful women can be self-centered, and let's face it, it's difficult to maintain all the claptrap of beauty in a place like Kenya, especially on safari . . . *Mrs. Warner.*"

I laughed, even as I pushed my hair back off my face, conscious that my eyes must be swollen and red, and any semblance of makeup had gone by the way hours ago. I would certainly qualify as not beautiful, definitely at this moment.

"A woman who wants children," he continued, "and who can take care of her children and herself in case something unforeseen happens to me. Someone who is brave and has a sense of adventure, and you certainly qualify in those characteristics. All right, turnabout. What attracted you to Phillip?"

I thought for a moment. "He just had such a joyful life. I met him at the club when the members invited the newly arrived Americans. He seemed more mature than the guys on the project or the ones I had dated back home. In fact, I was engaged to one from back home when I met Phillip, but before the evening was over, I was in love with him. He didn't drink a lot like so many of the men at the club, and he didn't leave me to play darts. He seemed interested in talking with me. It's hard to explain, and you're the only person who's ever asked me. His parents seem to approve, and so we were married. It might not have lasted into middle-age —

who knows? But we had a good time together." I felt tears forming in my eyes, thinking of Phillip, and I looked away before Ian noticed.

"And what about Marcello?" he asked, as I had been expecting him to.

"Do you mean what attracted me to him? Am I eager to see him?"

"But it looks like I'll have to wait till later to share secrets," said Ian. "We're almost at the entrance to the hotel."

I glanced up and saw a lorry coming around a curve heading straight for us. It was carrying a coffin.

Chapter 16

Joseph swung the vehicle across the lane, blocking the lorry, and slammed on the brakes. I couldn't stop myself from screaming, as we seem to be only inches from it.

"Stay here," Ian ordered, reaching into his knapsack for his badge, and sliding open the van's door. Joseph was already out, his badge in his hand.

Joseph went to the driver's side, and Ian to the passenger side, both holding up police badges. Even from my vantage point, I could see the frightened look in the driver's eyes, which seemed to be like huge white marbles in his dark face. Without being asked, he handed Joseph what I assumed was his driver's license. Joseph held it, while the driver got down from the cab, hands up.

"You can put your hands down," Ian said, coming around to frisk the driver, while Joseph held a pistol on him.

"Ain't got nothing to steal," the driver mumbled.

"We're not trying to rob you, unless you're carrying a load of gold on the back of your lorry," Ian said.

"Gold? Nothing in that coffin but a body, and I need to get him across the lake to Kisumu."

"We'll settle matters in just a moment," Ian assured him, having patted down the driver. He shook his head, and Joseph handed the pistol over to Ian. Joseph and the driver climbed up onto the back of the lorry and untied the ropes that held the simple wooden coffin in place. "Can you open it?" Joseph asked.

"Not unless you've got a crowbar," the driver said.

Ian came back to the van where we did indeed have a crowbar, and handed it up to Joseph. After a few screeching sounds of nails pulling free from wood, the lid came free, and Joseph stepped back, holding his nose.

"Do you have papers, a receipt for hauling this body?" Joseph asked.

"What do I need papers for? He's my cousin, and he got killed in a fight, and I'm taking him for his burial."

"I don't think the health authorities, or customs would let him make the trip all the way to Europe, judging by the smell," Ian said, handing up a hammer. "There's no false bottom, and no stencil directions," Joseph said.

Joseph soon had the lid nailed down securely and both men climbed down off the back of the lorry. "Our apologies," he said to the driver. "We're looking for a body, but this is not it. You can be on your way." He handed the driver his license, and Joseph and Ian got back in the van and backed it up to turn into the hotel entrance.

"I hope we haven't blown our cover as tourists on Safari," Ian said.

Chapter 17

Joseph turned into the driveway of the Mountains of the Moon hotel, stopped at the front entrance, and slid open the door so Ian could help me down. Before anyone could come out to collect our luggage, Joseph set down our cases and knapsack, and slammed shut the rear door to the van, leaving the rifles inside and out of sight.

He had acted so quickly that he was already standing by the driver side by the time a porter came out for our baggage. I noticed that Ian had the binoculars slung around his neck.

"Tomorrow morning we set off at eight, *bwanna*," Joseph said, "unless that is too early." He looked from Ian to me, waiting for objection or confirmation.

"Is that too early for you, dear?" Ian asked me. Then, without waiting for my answer, he turned back to Joseph. "Better make it eight-thirty. Josie likes a leisurely breakfast first. Maybe we can have a walk around before breakfast to see if we spot any animals."

"Maybe some birds," I suggested, going along with our charade of being ordinary people on safari, although the last thing I wanted to do early in the morning was tramp around in the mist and fog that were likely to come off the nearby lakes, and brush against wet grass. "There are some beautiful birds in East Africa," I concluded truthfully.

"What about the food in the hamper?" Joseph asked.

"Hand me a couple of the sandwiches," Ian said, stuffing them in his knapsack. "Give the rest to any of the drivers you see."

Joseph nodded. *"Muzri,"* he said in Swahili, using the expression Europeans and Africans alike sometimes used. He got into the van and drove away. The porter stood waiting, and I wondered how much of our conversation he had understood—probably nothing except the word *"Muzri,"* but I was becoming supersensitive to people who might be spies.

The porter picked up our bags and trotted along ahead of us into the hotel lobby, his bare feet slapping on the tile floor.

Ian stepped up to the desk. "A reservation for Mr. and Mrs. Alan Warner," he said.

"Yes, sir. Your safari guide booked the standard room for you. That comes with dinner and breakfast, of course."

"Does it have a view?" Ian asked.

"All our rooms have some view, sir," the clerk responded, with just a hint of condescension.

"Do you have a room at the end of the building, facing the mountains?" Ian asked, and I thought he was overplaying the tourist just a bit. "We'd like privacy too. I'll pay extra to get what we want. This trip is a belated honeymoon, and we want to get the most out of our safari." He put his arm around me.

After a moment of consulting the ledger and a layout of the hotel, the clerk pointed to a corner room. "I think this satisfies all your desires, sir," he said, with a knowing glance at us. I felt a little embarrassed and annoyed at his smirk, but then I reasoned that, at least as far as this man was concerned, we were what we pretended to be. Ian laid some bills on the desk, and I saw that the clerk pocketed two and put the remainder in the till, before writing a receipt.

We followed the porter up the single flight of stairs and down the hall to our room. He unlocked the door, handed the key with a huge metal ball hanging from it to Ian, and walked across the room to open the curtains, revealing a breathtaking view of the mountains. He opened the closet, took out a luggage rack and opened it, setting my suitcase on it, then opened the bathroom door to demonstrate. Ian gave it a cursory inspection while I stood taking in the view, handed the Porter two shillings, and closed the door after him.

Ian joined me at the window, putting his arm around my waist, and leaning his head over to touch mine, just as if we were being spied on and had to continue playing our part.

"I don't know what kind of view the standard room had, but this is marvelous," I said. "Thank you for making the change."

"I'm glad you like it," he said. His body touching mine from shoulder to hip, his hand clasping my waist, brought an image of lying beside him on the big bed. He turned me so that I faced him, and I thought for a moment he was going to kiss me. I stepped away from him.

He laughed lightly. "Later, Mrs. Warner, when you're ready. I changed the room for several reasons. First, the police and civil servants always get the standard room, so when I ask for something better and paid for it, he dropped any suspicions he might have had about our being police, and took us for wealthy tourists. Second, that standard room would have had a lot of foot traffic passing by it at all hours. At this location, there should be only us and whoever is assigned the room across the hall, if anyone. That way, nothing will be suspicious if we hear footsteps. There's also an exit in case of fire — or for any other reason that we might need to escape quickly."

"You seem to have thought of everything," I said. "I'm impressed."

"I'm good at my job. That's why I was chosen for this investigation. The view is important too. In this direction, we can see the mountains." He pointed to the other window.

"That one overlooks the parking lot, so we can see who comes and goes. The clerk thought he was giving us the second best room, but for our purposes the view of the parking lot is just what we want."

"Where is Joseph's room?" I asked.

"He's staying in the quarters with the other guides. It's demeaning for a policeman of his caliber, but he accepts it. It gives him an excuse to have a rifle with him, and he can talk to other tour guides and even some of the hotel staff, and he may get some valuable information just by listening." Ian reached for my hand, guiding me toward the door. "Let's go down and have a sundowner. Your usual?"

"Gin and tonic."

"A perfect drink for the tropics, might even help with malaria. They'll probably serve us roast beef and potatoes, or perhaps some fried tilapia, both of which are safe. So, *Mrs. Warner*," he emphasized my pretend name and title, just as a newly married man would do—just as Phillip had done. "Shall we go enjoy what this fine old hotel has to offer. It may be a good while before dinner. Do you want one of the sandwiches now?"

"Yes, thanks. Let's share one"

After we ate the sandwich, we freshened up and changed clothes before we went down.

Ian locked the door behind us and took my hand, as we walked along the corridor down the steps, across the lobby and outside to a tiny table. I noticed that he had not turned in the big key at the front desk, as guests were supposed to do when they were out of their rooms. He had also hung the "do not disturb" sign on the doorknob. As he pulled out one of the white, painted metal chairs for me, he answered my unspoken question in a quiet voice: "I want them to think were still inside. Maybe they won't connect the couple having drinks on the lawn with the couple who are supposed to be making love to each other on the big bed."

As he pushed my chair into place, he bent over and dropped down to kiss me on the back of my neck, soft and warm, in the cool early evening air. I had a fleeting, enticing image of the two of us entwined on the bed, basking in each other's arms.

I stopped myself thinking such thoughts. Just hours ago we had been near death. Any romance now was pretense. The scrape of Ian's chair against the stones of the patio veranda ended my thoughts—at least for now. He raised his hand for service, and the waiting African attendant came to our table. His white *kanzu* came down to his ankles, his feet were bare, and on his head he wore a maroon fez. He said nothing, waiting for our order.

" Two gin and tonics, *tafidali?*" he asked the waiter as he held up two fingers.

The waiter left, returning quickly with a tray carrying two glasses, a bottle of gin, and two bottles of tonic water— along with the usual bowl of nuts. Ian signed the chit, and the waiter expertly poured gin in each glass, then the tonic water, adding a wedge of lime to the rim of each glass. There was no ice, nor did I expect any.

The waiter bowed and left, and we lifted our glasses and said, "Cheers." Ian added, "To a successful enterprise."

I sipped my drink and took in the beautiful, serene setting, basking in the perfection of this moment. A clump of Frangipani bloomed nearby, its wonderful fragrance like that of tiny gardenias, filled the air, and I knew that I would always try to recapture in memory that fragrance from East Africa. A Jacaranda tree bloomed purple against the misty blue outlines of the mountains. The grass was cut immaculately, as if someone had used a measuring stick throughout, with not a stray leaf or twig marring its green perfection. It was edged expertly beside a pebbled pathway that led to flower beds. Stately Triatoma, which my grandmother called "red hot poker's," because of their flame-like flower heads, lorded it over a lush bed of Agapanthus, lilies of the Nile.

Into this serenity ran two small monkeys, chasing each other and pausing as if they were playing tag. I laughed. "Now we are back in Africa. Everything else here could be at a Grand Hotel anywhere in the world."

"Anywhere there is ample rainfall and servants to be hired for low wages," Ian said thoughtfully. "You are seeing the last and the best of the British Empire."

"It's not what anyone in America would think of when they hear the word Africa, and it's not what I expected either. I don't know why we're staying here tonight, but I'm glad we are."

"We couldn't have gone any further tonight. The roads are dangerous enough by daylight, but at night they are death traps. We don't want more than one scare per day. But it has its other purposes too."

We sipped our drinks for a while, and poured the remaining tonic water into our glasses.

"I wish this could go on forever," I said, "the beauty of the grounds and the mountains, the peace and quiet, and —"

Before I could say "and good company," a very British voice said, "Jumbo! May we join you?" A red-faced man, whom I took to be an upcountry farmer, and a buxom woman in a shirtwaist dress and cardigan, approached our table, both carrying drinks in their hands.

Short of being rude, we had no choice. Whenever Europeans encountered each other anywhere in East Africa, they talked together over drinks and dinner.

Ian gestured toward a nearby table and chairs just like ours. "Of course. Pull up a chair—and the table."' He set down his glass and rose to help the man bring over a nearby table and chairs, and we all seated ourselves, facing each other as much as we could, given that both tables were round.

Ian held out his hand to shake those of the others. "I'm Alan Warner, and this is my bride, Josie."

"Toby and Hilary Bissell. We have a farm up in the rift, with a grand view of Mount Longonot. I'll miss it when we have to leave."

"Congratulations, you two!" his wife trilled. "I was watching you through the doorway, while the barman was fixing our drinks, and I had already guessed that you were newlyweds, the way you look at each other and . . ." she hesitated and then went on, ". . . touch each other."

I felt my face grow hot, as embarrassed as if we had been doing something wrong. We'd been spied on, but at least we played our parts well. I felt her staring at me, and I tried to think of something to say, but I needn't have worried about conversation. Toby Bissell took care of that.

"I reckon we have two years at the most before we have to sell out. I won't get much for the farm, unless some wealthy Arabs buy it for the view. There's some talk of the government buying up some of the big farms and dividing them up into small "*shambas*" to reward their loyal followers. Ungrateful lot! We've brought them civilization—roads and railroads, doctors and hospitals, schools, churches and the rule of law. And what thanks do we get? Not a bit! They tried to scare us off with Mao Mao, but that didn't work. Now her Majesty's government is pulling the rug out from under us legally."

He picked up his glass and took a long drink. I had heard this kind of talk before, and I knew what was coming, but I couldn't think of any remark that would open a different line of conversation.

"You mark my words," he went on, "you come back here five years after independence and you won't recognize the place. Everything will need painting or repairing. Broken windows will be boarded up, anything that can be carried away will be stolen, and cattle will be grazing on this lawn."

His wife reached forward and touched his arm. "We must look on the bright side, Toby." She directed her next words to me. "It breaks my heart to leave. I have spent all my life out here, and I'll be leaving a place I love and a life I love, to go to a cold rainy place, to live in a small stone house, with only an occasional servant to come in to help out."

Toby picked up the story again. "We've been thinking of Australia. The Johanssons are planning to go there, but going that far away is a big decision. And did you know there's a hotel on the coast that's for sale for only six thousand quid?"

I had heard so many people at the club talking about where they would go when they left Africa that I paid little heed to what was being said. Suddenly, Hilary broke in.

"You look so familiar, Josie. I've seen you somewhere. I just can't think where." She frowned in concentration, biting her lower lip.

"People often tell me I remind them of someone," I said with a little laugh. "They never say I remind them of Elizabeth Taylor or Ava Gardner or the Queen. It's always their cousin or their aunt."

She shook her head. "No, it's not that. I've seen you. It'll come to me."

"Maybe we were sitting at nearby tables having lunch at the new Stanley, or having tea while we waited for our husbands," I suggested.

"It was outdoors somewhere. I remember you looking so cool while I was sweating up a storm. Do you and your husband go to rugby matches?"

Ian broke in, sensing what was coming as clearly as I did. "I'm not much of a rugby player, I'm afraid. How about you, Toby?"

Toby laughed. "Any team that depends on me would be counted out early on. My muscles went on leave ages ago. Besides, the farm keeps me busy."

Hilary was not diverted. "Maybe you were there by yourself, or with someone else."

Ian chuckled and put his arm around me. "She dated a few other fellows, but once I met her, that put paid to anyone else."

"Terrible what happened to young Phillip What's his name," Toby said "and deuced strange as well."

I had known this was coming from the moment rugby was mentioned, but his words were like a huge icicle piercing my heart.

I wanted to stop Toby from talking about Phillip's accident, and I wanted to stop Hilary from thinking too much about what I may have said to her that day at the rugby match. Everyone has something they've done or some incident that they would rather forget, and Hilary was no exception. She had been flustered and apologetic that day, and, in a way, I hated to bring it up, but I had to stop her. I had to keep to my role as Ian's wife. "You look familiar, too," I said. "And I'd been trying to remember where I'd seen you, but your mentioning the rugby match brought it back. You'll be pleased to know that I was able to get the stains out of my slacks."

Her eyes widened and her face turned a deep embarrassed red. "Oh, I'm glad. I was such a clumsy oaf."

111

"No real harm done," I said consolingly. "It was a little embarrassing walking around in damp slacks that had a slightly orange cast in the seat, but I was just relieved that the bottle of squash just squirted out instead of breaking when you dropped it and it hit the cement. Let's not think any more about that day. I had almost forgotten the incident until you mentioned that we had met."

She nodded, and took a long gulp of her scotch and water.

I had stopped her, but not Toby. He went on relentlessly. "A damned dicey affair, that," he mused. "I've driven the escarpment more times than I can count, and I never had any trouble, except once the driver of a slow lorry couldn't seem to get it into gear, and I thought for a moment he was going to roll back over me, but the booger made the crest just in the nick of time, and then he was rolling fast down the other side. Could be a runaway lorry hit Phillip's car, or maybe somebody gave him a nudge over the side on purpose."

He paused, and I was hoping Ian would intervene with some remark that would change the subject, but it was obvious that Toby was about to make a point.

"I heard somebody say at the club that the police are having another look at the car, but that lot don't know which end is up. They couldn't solve a crime even if they committed it themselves. Oh well, water over the dam."

I felt Ian's hand tighten on my arm, and I knew he was seething at Toby's insult to police. I thought about Joseph, who was not only a superb driver, but a competent investigator. So far, Toby and Hilary had not asked our occupations, or how long we'd been married, and I realized that we hadn't prepared our answers. I had to depend on Ian to supply the answers before the questions were asked.

The sun was setting, silhouetting the mountains in dark blue, and the air had grown cool. I shivered slightly, wishing I had brought my cardigan down from the room.

"Getting chilly, darling?" Ian asked. He looked at his watch. "Why don't we go on in and have an early dinner?" He stood, and pulled back my chair.

"What do you say, old girl?" Toby asked Hilary. Then, making the decision for both of them, he said, "Join you in a sec, and I'll have the boy bring our next round to the table."

We followed the waiter to a table by the window with a view of the garden. It was set with a damask tablecloth and matching napkins in rings. A bowl of pink roses stood in the center of the table, beside a hurricane lamp with a lighted candle inside. Beside each plate was the usual array of cutlery and glasses that I had come to expect of even the most isolated of hotels. The waiter helped me get seated, and placed a printed menu card in front of us. I knew this was not really a choice, only a listing of what the evening's dinner included. I could probably have written it myself, as it seemed to be the same across East Africa. The soup was cream of leek, which I liked, and the fish was fried tilapia from the nearby lakes. The entrée was roast beef, broiled tomato halves and fried potatoes. For dessert—or as it was called in East Africa, "sweet" or "pudding"—there was chocolate cream Brulé followed by cheese and fruit, if anyone got that far.

The waiter had just set down a basket of bread, wrapped in a linen cloth, and a bowl of cold butter balls imprinted in a crisscross pattern, when the Bissells came in, followed by the barman bearing a tray of drinks.

The barman set down a tumbler half-full with what I took to be scotch in front of each of the Bissells and a carafe of water between them. Toby picked up his glass and downed half the scotch. "I think water kind of ruins a good scotch," he said with a laugh. "This will hold me until the bubbly arrives."

"What are you celebrating?" I asked. He had certainly seemed to foresee a gloomy future.

"It's congratulations to you two newlyweds. Your good company."

I took this to mean we'd be listening to his rants without interrupting. Ian smiled and said "Thank you. So what brings you this far away from the farm?"

"Thought we'd have a last could look around East Africa, the way we want to remember it. We brought the car across the lake on the ferry, but we plan to go back all the way on land. We took in Rwanda and Burundi, and they are not as advanced as Uganda and certainly not Kenya. Plan to go into the Congo, up to Lake Kivu, which used to be a pretty little place, and follow the River to Leopoldville. I went there once years ago, but it's different now that the Belgians are all gone."

I felt Ian's thigh pressing against mine under the table, and while I didn't know exactly what his signal meant, I did know that we were going to keep on listening to this man as long as he talked.

Chapter 18

"What was it like?" Ian asked Toby, as he turned back the edges of the linen covering the bread basket, and passed it around, followed by the dish of butter. When the basket got back to him, he took a slice, attempted to spread butter on it, but failed, only succeeding in rolling the ball along the bread, picking up loose crumbs. I had long ago given up on spreading cold balls of butter. "We've given some thought to going into the Congo ourselves."

"Oh, don't go!" Hilary exclaimed. "I was frightened the entire time. We were never out of sight of Africans with *pangas,* and even a few with guns, and I thought every moment might be my last."

Toby left his bread untouched on the small plate, while he held the tumbler in both hands and stared into it, then looked up, first at Ian and then at me. "I wouldn't go if I were you. It's a cesspit of a country. The Belgians picked up and left without a warning—at least that's what they thought, but somebody got wind of the evacuation and cleaned out the national bank. Probably a member of the government, or maybe the banker himself. He's disappeared, and so has the money, but there are rumors that it's being smuggled out of the country bit by bit, and the same thing with the payroll money for the Katanga mines. A suspiciously large number of Congolese banknotes have turned up in other parts of Africa and even in Europe, especially Brussels. The money is about worthless now, of course, but the gold is something else. Gold never loses its value."

The waiter brought our soup just then, smooth and creamy with bits of green leeks blended throughout. Both Hilary and I ate our soup as we had been taught to, dipping it carefully away from us and not slurping. Ian ate rapidly, faster than I'd seen him eat, and I knew he was eager to hear more of Toby's story. Toby tore his slice of bread into pieces and pushed them into his soup with his spoon, and began to dig them out soggy, more like a casserole than a soup.

As the waiter took away our soup dishes and replaced them with plates of fried fish, the barman arrived with four glasses and a bottle of champagne. He expertly popped the cork and poured the champagne carefully down the side of the glasses so that it didn't foam up. While we clicked our glasses in toast and sipped champagne, the waiter went around the table deboning our fish, cutting off the heads, with their wide-open eyes, and their tails, and lifting out the offending bones. He carried away all the debris, which I suspected would end up as fish bisque along with any leftover bits of fish. Africans seldom wasted food.

Even after a year in Africa, I still had some difficulty using the arc shaped fishing knife, but I managed. The Tilapia was delicious, white and soft, flaking apart at the slightest touch of the knife. I was still eating when Ian pushed back his plate and asked, "How do they smuggle gold without getting caught?"

Toby pushed back his plate and reaching his finger into his mouth, he retrieved an errant fishbone and laid it on his plate. "The Congo is a real hell hole," he said downing the last of his champagne as if it could wash away the image his words conjured. "Once it had broad, clean streets, sparkling-white, government buildings, and big graceful houses set in palm groves. A man could make a good living managing a copper mine or working with other minerals, including uranium. The rubber plantations flourished then, too. In that hot, wet climate, things rust overnight, so it was a struggle to keep it all in tip top shape. Now, nobody even tries."

He paused, picked up the tumbler, saw that it was empty of Scotch, and signaled the barman for a refill. He glanced around the table. "Anyone else?"

Ian shook his head. "Josie and I have an early morning game drive so we'll be going up soon, but I want to hear what you have to say about the Congo. It fascinates me."

Toby took a good swallow of his Scotch, and went on. "The minute the Belgians left, Africans moved into their houses, and I can't blame them for that, but they now act as if their employers are gone, and they don't have to work. Every building needs paint, the streets are full of potholes, and nobody bothers to fill them—*and*, they don't do any repaving. There's no public works department, because there are no taxes collected, and nobody is really in charge. They never learned to do things for themselves to improve their lot. Anything that hits the ground stays there and when the rains come, the whole mess—banana peels, coconuts, dead animals, even a few corpses of Africans—gets washed into the river and clogs up all the boat landings. Stray dogs tear at garbage, dead bodies, and each other. The stink would knock you off your feet."

He paused and wiped his hand across his forehead. I shifted my upper body so I could look at Ian, at least in profile, while still keeping my thigh touching his. With one hand he tapped his thigh impatiently and it vibrated slightly against mine. I knew he wanted to hear more about the gold smuggling, not so much about the nauseating condition of the Congo.

But Toby would not be hurried. "The mines used to support the country and make a hell of a profit as well. I worked there myself, supervising the African workers, and sometimes having to turn my hand to the hard work as well. My main job was keeping the machinery running. Now, it's finished. Nobody bothered to maintain the mines, and they are dangerous as hell. But the others are still there. The Russians and the Chinese—and some clever Arabs—are probably already making deals with African warlords to buy the mines for pennies on the pound, and what little money comes into the Congo will be out and on its way to Switzerland as fast as you can say Jack Robinson."

"What's the story about the gold smuggling?" Ian asked, when Toby paused to take another drink. "I heard some rumors about it, too, but nothing definite."

"Can't help you there, old man. My information comes from my friend Charlie, but it's nothing definite, nothing to report to the United Nations."

"What's Charlie's source of information?" Ian asked, and I thought he was sounding too much like a policeman gathering evidence, rather than a tourist chatting over drinks.

Toby didn't seem to notice, and Hilary had long lapsed into silence, almost asleep from the effects of her drinks. I'd been so caught up in Toby's narrative that I'd scarcely noticed that we'd gone through our entrées and little metal pans of crème brûlée with crested sugar atop that had been set down before us.

I picked up my spoon and broke the crust on my brûlée. Aside from the caramelized sugar on top, the brûlée was fairly tasteless, but I ate it anyway. We said no to the cheese course, although I thought it might have been a good idea to stash some in my purse for the next day's lunch. Cups of coffee and a pitcher of hot milk were brought to finish our meal, and I wasn't surprised when Toby ordered brandy to go with his coffee.

As impatient as Ian was to have the rest of the story, he said no more until the coffees had been finished.

Toby seemed ready to continue. "Charlie and I both worked at the mine in Katanga. I had enough of it after a while, and, by that time, on a trip to Mombasa, I met Hilary. She inherited a farm, and I bought the beginnings of a purebred herd of cattle and one of sheep. My animals always win prizes at the royal show."

Here, even Hilary seemed to sense that the story was going off the rails. She cleared her throat and said, "We can invite them to the farm later, dear. Right now, tell them about Charlie."

Toby nodded. "Yes, well, we dropped in on Charlie, and at first I didn't recognize him. He was sitting in a rocking chair on the veranda of his house—about the only one anywhere around him that had any semblance of maintenance done. His dog was curled up at his feet, and he held a rifle in one hand. Where he got it, I don't know. Maybe it was left over from the days when he managed the mine. He stood up and pointed it at us until I called him by name. Then he laid it across his chair and came down the steps to meet us. His beard was down to midway on his chest and his hair was past his shoulders, black and greasy. He needed a bath pretty badly. I said, "Looks like you've gone native, old boy," and he shrugged and said that the pipes were rusted out and the city water system was kaput, so he paid his house boy to bring him cans of water. He was the only European I saw in his neighborhood, and he was ready to leave. Someone had stolen his car, but it wouldn't have made a difference anyway, as there was no petrol station near him. Africans had siphoned off the petrol out of the abandoned stations, and the last tanker truck that went in turned over. The petrol was set afire and the whole thing exploded, going up like a bomb."

I could feel Ian's tense impatience, so I said, "So, what did Charlie tell you, and what happened to him?"

"Charlie said he had something suspicious to tell me, and waved us to a seat on the veranda. I told him I was taking him out of there, and we had to get going so we could clear the border well before dark. I was pretty sure I had enough petrol to make it to Kasese or even here. Charlie said he'd tell me on the way, then, but he had to take his dog and his rifle along. I didn't think the border guards would let a rifle pass going either way, and I wasn't too keen on having that mangy dog riding in the rover, even though it's seen better days on the farm. But Charlie was my friend, and I wanted to rescue him, so I agreed."

Toby paused, drained the last of his coffee, and tipped up the tumbler to get the last few drops of Scotch before he went on. "Charlie said he would be just a minute, and he came back carrying a beat-up, brown, leather briefcase and a leash for the dog. He was still wearing the same stained tan shirt and shorts and sandals made out of rubber innertubes, just what the Africans wear. I asked him if he didn't want to bring along a change of clothing. He patted the briefcase and said he had some clean underwear that he would put on after he finally got a chance to get a bath, and his bank book, a couple of ledgers, address book, and his passport that was curved to fit his rear pocket. He said everything else had been stolen except for the things he used all the time, like the bed and table and chairs, and he'd leave it behind gladly, knowing it would be out of there before nightfall.

"Well, between Charlie and the dog, I thought Hilary and I would pass out from the fumes. I kept all the windows on the Rover wide open, and turned the wings to bring in extra air current. As soon as we got going, I asked him what the suspicious incident was. He said a Belgian—or maybe a German, he wasn't sure—came to the house one day, offered to ship his body back to Europe and pay for a funeral if he died within the next year. Charlie is no fool, and he knows that when a total stranger offers you something he claims is free, you better run the other way. Charlie told him he wasn't planning to die within the next year." Toby laughed, a laugh that turned into a strangled kind of cough that made his red face even redder. Finally, he got control of himself and went on. "Charlie asked the man if they'd come into the Congo to get him and the man said no, they'd make plans to get him into Uganda. Take him to Kasese, and they'd even supply his casket."

"Did they mention anything about shipments — how often they sent bodies to Europe and so on?" Ian asked.

Toby shook his head. "But what else could it be? Charlie was eager to get out of the Congo, but he didn't much relish sitting around Kasese with someone planning for him to die within a year. We had seen several trucks carrying caskets, more than I would have expected."

"We were almost run over by a lorry carrying a casket, just outside the entrance to the hotel," Ian said. Actually, we had blocked the lorry, but I knew Ian had a reason for lying, and I didn't correct him. "Where is Charlie now?" he asked.

"Somewhere in or around Kasese, as far as I know. He had to give up his rifle at the border, when the United Nations chappies stopped us, but Charlie passed it over willingly. He said he had no ammunition for it anyway, but had just kept it to warn off people. I dropped him off at a cheap hotel and paid for one night in advance, the only way they'd take him, and I couldn't blame them. Charlie said he had plenty of money but he just couldn't get at it, said all the years he'd been out in the Congo he'd sent money to his sister back in the UK and she'd invested it, as well as living on it, and now it amounted to a tidy sum. He'd also set up a savings account in a Kasese bank, but hadn't been able to bring any of that money into the Congo. I didn't know how much of his story to believe, but I figured I could stand to lose the cost of a night's hotel and breakfast."

At this point, much to my surprise, Hilary spoke up. "It was worth paying whatever it cost just to get him out of the car. I thought he was crazy, if you want to know. Living alone in the Congo, seeing people get shot down in the street right in front of you, not knowing what kind of food would be available the next day, if any, and not having even the simple things we take for granted, like bath water and soap. It would certainly drive *me* crazy.

"Charlie told me to come around to his hotel the next morning and he'd repay me. I half expected him to hit me up for a loan, but we went anyway. When we got to the hotel, he wasn't there, and the desk clerk said he'd gone out early, leaving his dog. The dog lay contentedly on the floor near the door. When Charlie came in, I hardly recognized him. He'd had his hair and beard trimmed, and was wearing some decent looking clothes. He handed me a handful of shillings, and tipped the desk clerk for minding his dog and — I presume — getting it washed, since it didn't stink anymore. I asked him if he wanted to come along with us, but he said no. He thought he'd see what kind of job he might pick up at the mines here. Also, he would try to locate the man who offered him a free funeral and try to find out what that was all about."

"That sounds dangerous," Ian said. "Why doesn't he just leave well enough alone and go home to be with his sister?"

"He said he would push off eventually," said Toby, "even if it means having to put the dog in quarantine when he gets home."

"Josie and I may end up there after we've seen enough animals," Ian said. "If we run across him, shall I have a go at trying to persuade him to leave Africa, or is it a hopeless case?"

"His last name is Hill. He's always said he'd leave Africa feet first, but I don't think he's fool enough to get involved with whoever wants a body of a European. God knows there are enough bodies of Africans in and around the Congo to fill up caskets as fast as they can be built."

Ian stood and helped me stand beside him. He stifled a yawn with his other hand and said, "It's been fascinating talking with you, Toby. Maybe we'll see you tomorrow morning after we make our game drive and have breakfast, if you're still here."

We said our good nights amid compliments and best wishes, and headed for our room. My head whirled with the images Toby had described, and I couldn't help thinking that Ian and I were in some ways as foolish as Charlie, heading into the dangerous unknown.

Chapter 19

Ian and I said nothing to each other as we walked back to our room. He guided me along with his hand on the small of my back, since I was a bit lightheaded from champagne. I welcomed his strength and stability. As I came out of the bathroom in my nightgown, I said, "I thought Toby Bissell would never shut up. He really likes to hear himself talk, and he never gives Hilary a chance to get in a word in edgewise."

Picking up his own toiletries and nightwear, Ian said, "He is a bit of a blowhard, but in the midst of all that blather were some pretty graphic descriptions, which was useful information. His friend, Charlie, is savvy or he wouldn't have lasted so long in the Congo. He confirmed that the gold smugglers are still looking for European bodies, which means that they still have substantial amounts of gold—and perhaps other valuables, even uranium—that they need to transport to Europe."

When Ian came out of the bathroom, I was seated at the vanity brushing my hair. He came to stand behind me and our glances met in the mirror.

"I think we need to forget our morning game drive and get on to Kasese to look up Charlie Hill. He has a passport and a bank savings book, two things which are very valuable almost anywhere, and he's carrying what he thinks are some valuable documents—in addition to his having been contacted by the smugglers. I think he can help us, in return for police protection and a lift to Nairobi."

I stopped brushing my hair and laid the brush down. "I agree."

"Would you like me to brush your hair?" he asked. He lifted a lock of my hair and slid it across his index finger.

"No thanks. That went out with the Victorian age, when women had long flowing tresses and their hair was seen mostly braided or in a bun."

"I like yours just the way it is," he said.

I was exhausted, but I was too keyed up by the day's happenings to sleep, and by what I dreaded to come in the next few days. I hadn't needed Phillip's pistol, and I wondered if I could make myself shoot another human being. I feared that I would soon find out.

We got into bed, tucked in the mosquito net beneath the edge of our mattress on each side, and lay stiffly beside each other.

"You could turn back from here," Ian suggested in the darkness. "We could pretend we had a quarrel and you're leaving me in anger."

"No," I whispered. "I should never have started on this journey, but now that I've come this far, I'll see it to the end."

"I thought that's what you'd say. From Kasese on to the end, they'll be no more pretending to be tourists. Joseph and I clearly will be police, and will be sending for reinforcements and a helicopter to take us out in a hurry if things go really bad. I'll protect you as much as I can."

"And I'll protect myself as much as I can."

In that moment, he rolled over onto his side and pulled me against him, one hand in my hair, guiding my face close to his for a kiss.

It was more comforting than sexual. I snuggled against him. I felt my fear of what was to come slowly subside.

Just then, there was a flash of lighting followed by a great crash of thunder. I sat up with a jerk.

"Are you frightened of storms?" he asked.

"No. Actually, I like to watch storms." I tore the mosquito net free of the mattress and slid out, walking barefoot, to pull aside the heavy draperies that shielded our window. Lightning flashed with a brilliant illumination of the whole sky beyond the mountains, and was followed almost immediately by a roll of thunder that seemed to go on and on.

Ian's arm was around my shoulder. "I'm not surprised that you like thunderstorms. So do I, and I rather had suspected that you would be that kind of woman. Otherwise, you wouldn't be standing here wrapping yourself in the sound and light of it."

I leaned against him and we stood sharing the spectacle, until the thunder and lightning moved away and only came to us as faint reminders. Then, great drops of rain began to fall, lashing against the window, at first, and then settling to a steady downpour. We got back into bed, and I fell asleep almost immediately,

The next thing I knew, it was morning, and Ian was already up, bathed and dressed, and taking in the inevitable tray of morning tea. I got my own bath and dressed quickly, forgoing the tea.

At breakfast, Ian sent a message to Joseph, and he came into the dining room almost immediately, already dressed and ready for our day's journey. Ian handed him a note, which Joseph took and tucked into his pocket, unopened, and left.

Despite the beautiful setting, I was as ready as they were to be on our way, and we were soon finished with breakfast, packed, and in the van. Joseph handed me a paper bag that held packets of sandwiches and chocolate biscuits, and then a tall thermos full of hot coffee. I stowed them behind me in the van, while Joseph pointed out a road. Ian shook his head and said we needed to go to Kasese first.

I had a slight headache and a growing tension as we neared Kasese. What might we face today? Yesterday there had been the poachers threatening to kill us, and the rampaging, grief-stricken elephant. The day before that I'd been held at gunpoint, and, the day before that, my car had been shot at. Each day had been worse than the day before.

I reached for Ian's hand for reassurance.

"We don't have to pretend being Mr. and Mrs. Warner much longer," he said.

I jerked my hand away. Had his affections and compliments all been part of an act?

Kasese had more Europeans than much of the surrounding area, because of the copper mine, but from the description of Charlie Hill, I thought we might be able to find him by asking around.

It was easier than that. We checked at the hotel dining room, where families occupied two of the tables, and then on the veranda. There sat our target: a man with trimmed gray beard and gray hair cropped just above his ears, not much shorter than my own hair. Amazingly, he wore a three-piece, gray business suit, totally unsuitable for the tropics, with a white shirt peeking out. As we approached, he was in the act of waving away two plates that stood on his table, but he was dining alone, and I wondered if he had two breakfasts.

"Charlie Hill?" Ian asked.

"Who wants to know?"

"Alan and Josie Warner. We met some friends of yours, Toby and Hilary Bissell, at the Mountains of the Moon hotel. They said we'd find you interesting, and might get some useful information from you."

"Sit, please. Would you like some coffee? I assume you had breakfast at the hotel. They put on a good one, I'm sure, just like this place. Whatever blunders we Brits have made in losing battles and empires, we still produce a jolly good breakfast—bacon and eggs, tomato, beans, toast with orange marmalade."

As the waiter removed the used plates and set down cups for our coffee, Charlie Hill went on, "It's darn good to have something in the morning more than a hard roll and a cup of weak coffee. Some Kippers would have been the icing on the cake. Lusty and I enjoyed the whole breakfast, even without kippers."

"Lusty?" Ian asked, with an upraised brow.

Charlie indicated the German Shepherd that slept peacefully at his feet.

"He doesn't look very lusty to me," Ian said, with a laugh.

"I got him when he was just a pup, and I thought about naming him Leo after the king who raped the Congo, but I respected my dog more than that. Half the dogs in Africa are named Simba for" lion," even though almost none of them have any resemblance to a lion. So I called him Rusty, but you know how the Africans sometimes transpose "L's" and "R's" so that Lori becomes Raleigh. My houseboy began to refer to him as" Lusty," and I decided the name was a good one. He's the only dog I've ever heard of named "Lusty."

"And is he Lusty?" Ian asked. He picked up his coffee, which the waiter had just poured, and sipped it. I did likewise, wondering where this conversation was leading.

"I took care of that matter years ago, and had him fixed. A lot of Africans are afraid of dogs, although some in the Congo probably are eating what few there are, now that food is so scarce, and I just couldn't see introducing any more creatures into that environment." He took a big sip of his

129

coffee and then said, "But you didn't come here to hear an old man natter on. What can I do for you?"

Ian lowered his voice, and I glanced around to see if anyone might be listening to us, but no one seemed to be paying us the slightest attention. "Toby Bissell didn't know why we're here, and never asked my business. I'm with CID, and my name is Ian Armstrong, not Warner. This lady"—he indicated me—"is not my wife. She's looking for someone, and we joined forces."

I noticed that Joseph had come in and taken a small table alone, close enough to hear us. Ian went on, "and the gentleman next to us who is pretending to be a tour guide is actually a skilled, high-ranking police officer."

"Then I suppose your business involves the Congo—the missing treasury?"

Ian, Joseph and I all nodded at the same time. Could it be this easy that we had found the very man who could lead us to our quarry?

"I can help you and you can help me," Charlie Hill said. "After I got tired of working in the mines, I went to work for the Congolese government. I speak passable French, I remember most of my English, as well as a smattering of several African languages, and I'm good with numbers. I was an underling, keeping records and making wire transfers to banks in Europe. Nobody paid much attention to me, and nobody knew that I was keeping records of my own. I never bragged, and never drank too much and let information slip, so they trusted me unthinkingly. When the troubles began and they left in a hurry, they forgot to kill me. I know how much was left in the treasury, and I know at least one of the names of the men who took it across the lake and brought it here—not exactly here, you understand, but in Uganda."

"Didn't you think of taking any of it for yourself?" Ian asked in amazement.

"How do you know I didn't?" Charlie asked, and then chuckled and shook his head. "I thought about it. But what would I do with gold bars and Congolese money? It was a risky business, and still is, with the police from half a dozen countries looking for the stuff. I've always lived in a thrifty way, and I still do." He gestured at his suit. "It's surprising what you can find in used clothing shops. I don't know why anybody would donate this, except it's scratchy as hell. Still, it's to make an impression on the man I have an appointment with."

"What man?" Ian asked.

"The one who offered to ship me home if I died within a year. I saw him on the street here yesterday, and I asked him if he could tell me more about it." He looked at his watch and added, "First watch I've had in years. Time seemed unimportant in the Congo. You're probably wondering why I stayed on so long."

"I certainly *am* wondering," I said.

He turned to me, almost as if in surprise that I had a voice. "At first I thought I could ride it out, and maybe even go to work for the African government that took over from the Belgians. You could count on one hand how many educated people there were in that government. The Europeans and Kenyans hate to leave, and a lot of them stay on, but they set up schools and colleges and hospitals, and trained Indians as well as Africans to run all the agencies and commissions and departments. Kenyatta will probably make a go of the government, but Lumumba won't. Anyway, by the time I concluded that I'd better get out, transportation was iffy. I couldn't take Lusty on our plane, and probably not on a bus. Having old Toby show up was a godsend."

"Why are you trusting us with all this information? Ian asked.

"I have to trust somebody, and I think you're telling me the truth about who you are. I'm ready to turn over all my information to the police, and make my way home to the UK from here. I want to lead a quiet life with my sister and not have to be looking over my shoulder wondering if someone is coming after me. If something happens to me out here, I want you to take my passport, my bankbook, and the Congolese record book out of the bank safe deposit box. Send the money to my sister whose address is in my passport, and turn the records over to Interpol or whoever should have them. You'll find the numbers of bank accounts in Switzerland mostly, with a few in Brussels, Cairo and even one in the Isle of Man. I had the money transfers for the thieves sent to those European accounts." He fished in his pocket for a moment and laid a card and some keys on the table. "This is the bank. The box number and code are on the back, and here are the keys."

"What would you have done if we hadn't come along this morning?" Ian asked.

"Destroy the card — I'm good at memorizing numbers — and kept the keys in my pocket. Nobody else would know what the keys were for." He stood, and looked down at his dog. "Stay, Lusty." Then he glanced quickly at each of the three of us. "I'm meeting the man a block away. Our meeting shouldn't take long. I wish I had a recorder or some way to get his words, but probably it's better I don't. I'm sure he'll frisk me, so I can't take a pistol, even if I had one. If I'm not back in half an hour, look for me. Go out of the hotel, across the street until you come to a street — really just an alley — that comes out on a little park. Wish me well."

Chapter 20

Joseph came over to our table and sat down. "Sir, with your permission, I think it's time we called for backup."

Ian nodded. "Go to it." He patted the pockets of his blue shirt. "I have the spare keys to the van, and the two-way radio."

"I have my pistol in my shoulder bag," I said.

Both men turned to look at me as if they'd forgotten I was there and that I had a weapon.

"Joanna, try to keep back behind me, or Joseph, as much as possible if trouble starts," Ian instructed me.

The tone of his voice told me that he was concerned about me and probably wished I wasn't there. "Yes, sir," I said.

Ian slapped his forehead and stood. "We are fools, all of us. That man is not going to give Charlie any information. Why would he? They're going to kill him and use him to cover the shipment of gold in the next coffin. Let's go!"

Ian had forgotten the keys and the card. I picked them up and dropped them into my shoulder bag.

Lusty had caught on before we did, or perhaps he heard some suspicious sound that was beyond our hearing. His head perked up, he leapt to his feet and raced off in the direction Charlie had gone.

Ian and Joseph outran me, and, by the time I reached the alley, I could see the results of what had happened. Joseph was holding an African against him, his pistol pointed at the man's cheek. A second African groveled on the ground, clutching at his genitals and moaning, heedless of the spreading pool of blood at his feet.

Ian squatted beside a badly injured Charlie, whose face was battered almost beyond recognition. I saw stark white bone sticking out through a rip in his coat sleeve, and I heard him say to Ian, "he knows," with a gesture toward the African Joseph had pinned against him.

Lusty, his brown fur red with blood in several places, lay beside Charlie, whimpering slightly.

Ian touched Lusty's head in a feeble effort to calm the helpless dog. With his other hand he had pulled the radio from his pocket and began to speak into it.

He briefly covered the speaker with his hand and said to me," I'm calling for help. Go get the van and park as close as you can outside." He patted his pocket and said, "Oh hell, I left the keys on the table back there."

I snatched the keys from my purse and showed them to him. I started running for the van and heard him say on his radio, "Ambulance and police. Now!"

I ran back past the hotel and to the parking lot where Joseph had conveniently parked the van so it was pointed, nose out. I'd never driven it, but I had to. I unlocked the door, slid in and inserted the ignition key on the third try. My hands were shaking so, I wondered if I could get the van in the right gear, but I managed it, and drove carefully up to the alley.

Joseph and his captive were out on the street, and as soon as I brought the van to a halt, Joseph slid open the side door and commanded the man to get in. "Pull up over there," he pointed farther up the street. "I'll guard the prisoner and you go tell the inspector where we are, although he can't miss it. We don't want to block the ambulance or the police, although their job is easy now."

"I won't have to drive the whole way, will I?"

He burst out laughing and shook his head. "Good God, no!"

As I got out of the van, an ambulance pulled up, its siren blaring and its lights flashing. Right behind it was a clearly marked police Land Rover, and behind that was a crowd, which had begun to gather to see what was going on.

I waited while Ian identified himself and Charlie, and as the medics lifted Charlie onto a stretcher and headed for the ambulance, Ian gently scooped up Lusty and took him to the ambulance as well, handing him up to one of the medics. He spoke briefly to the arriving police, who promptly took the other African away, and then Ian joined me. He took out his pistol and, as we walked the short distance to the van, he said, "You ride up front. Joseph will drive, and I'll sit in back with our prisoner who is going to tell us where to go. The locals probably want to arrest him for the attack on Charlie, but we have a bigger purpose for him."

As we left, Ian filled me in with what they had seen and assumed had happened. "The other African was holding Charlie while this sullen fellow beside me was beating him. Based on the blood on his back and shredded shirt, I'd guess that Lusty lunged for him and tore open all these deep scratches, which we are not going to attend to just yet, to let him know how it feels to be attacked instead of being the attacker. Then Lusty took on the other one, going first for his butt and then for his balls — pardon me, his genitals. They got quite a few scratches as well. You saw how he was reacting. Then this fellow beside me got his *panga* free from his belt and took on Lusty, I fear fatally. The police have the *panga* as evidence."

At the intersection, Joseph paused, and our captive pointed.

"Is he sure this is the right way?" Ian asked. "This looks like the road to the lodge on Lake Albert."

Joseph said something in a language I wasn't familiar with, and our captive shook his head. As I turned back to look at him, I saw that his eyes were large with fear. "No lie! Right way." He pointed again, and Joseph shifted gears and took the turn.

"What did you say to him that frightened him so?" I asked.

"I told him if he was lying to us, I'd see to it that Lusty scratched his balls the way he'd had his back scratched," Joseph said.

"I'm afraid Lusty won't be scratching anything anymore," Ian said.

"But this fellow doesn't know that," Joseph said.

It was the right way. We were back in the park, and after miles of driving, we came over a rise in the road, and down below us to the left was the Brown Log Lodge, with several vehicles parked beside it. I could even make out people sitting on the veranda. Three boats bobbed on the lake, and another pulled up to the dock. An African climbed out and secured the craft.

But before we reached the drive for the Lodge, the African pointed to the right. There, back in the trees, was a log stockade. To one side of it was what appeared to be a carpentry shop, with three freshly made coffins stacked up beside it, and sheets of plywood leaning against it. The stockade was big enough to hold several elephants. A very dark-skinned African, dressed in what appeared to be a Ranger uniform, stood guard with a rifle. He seemed unconcerned when our safari vehicle drove up, and I thought for a moment that our African prisoner, Daniel, had led us astray.

I was wrong.

Chapter 21

Joseph leaned over the seat and stuck a piece of duct tape over our prisoner's mouth and wrapped another piece around his legs. Ian pushed open the van door and we got out. The African's glance took in our clothing in the safari vehicle and pointed downhill. "Lodge over there. Not here," he said.

"You look so good in your uniform. Do you mind if my husband takes a picture of me with you?" I said, in what I hoped was a ditzy tourist voice, taking the camera out of my purse.

The African seemed doubtful, but stepped over beside me, and Ian indicated that he had his own camera. Out of the corner of my eye, I saw Joseph open the van door and slide out silently, then come around the back of the van. Just as Ian clicked the camera, Joseph struck the African guard with the butt of his pistol. The man slid to the ground and Joseph slapped the tape over the man's mouth and clicked handcuffs onto his wrists.

"Well done, Joseph," Ian said. "Now what do we do with him? If somebody comes out of the stockade looking for him, we're in trouble. "Where in the hell is Paddy? All hell can break loose here any minute."

As if in answer to his question, I heard the *whump, whump* of a helicopter. It cleared the treetops and settled down out in the clearing, spraying us with dust and debris. The engine shut down, and before the blades stopped turning, a half-dozen African police troops jumped down, dodging the blades. Patty O'Rourke followed them, and behind them was a young European man with a big camera.

"Three on each side of the stockade, and shoot anybody who comes out if they have a weapon." The police, Paddy and the cameraman approached us. The second vehicle, full of policeman from KCC, pulled into the drive and the men jumped out, ready for action. Paddy turned to the cameraman. "I'm going to repeat the instructions I gave you back at the office, with these three people as witnesses. You know Joseph, and you can take as many pictures of him as you want. These two are undercover, and their lives may be in danger if they are identified. You are *not* to take pictures of them, or even ask what their names are. If you do, I'll have you handcuffed, bound, and gagged, and your camera smashed. Do you agree?"

The cameraman nodded, and I saw his Adam's apple move up and down with his nervousness.

"That's not good enough. Say yes or no."

"I agree, the cameraman said."

"Stay by the van," Ian said. "I don't want anything to happen to you." He waved one of the African policemen over and told him, "Guard the *Memsahib* and the van. If the two prisoners try to get out, shoot them."

He turned back to me. "Do you have your pistol?"

I patted my purse. "Right here."

"Take it out and don't be afraid to use it if anybody tries to harm you, or gets too close. Stay here until we have cleared the stockade. When we bring Marcello out, you can talk to him — *if* he's still alive."

Ian walked away, just as a second helicopter approached. I moved around to the side of the van away from the stockade.

To my horror, I saw people running from the lodge and up the hill, pointing excitedly at the helicopters, running right into danger. "Get back! Get back!" I shouted. They couldn't hear me over the sound of the chopper. It landed. Three United Nations troops in khaki and blue jumped out. They looked about in uncertainly what to do, just as the first shooting began.

Paddy and Joseph stood one on each side of the stockade gate, and Paddy shouted, "Come out one by one with your hands up or I will blow up the place with you inside."

The first man ran out, but his hands weren't up. He was carrying a high-powered rifle that he didn't know how to use. He swung it wildly, spraying bullets every which way. They struck the van, sounding like hail on a tin roof, and the policeman who was guarding our prisoners was shot. If I had not moved from that side I would have been killed too. At the first shot, the cameraman who had been standing behind Joseph, hit the ground, clutching his camera underneath him. The shooter tripped over him, but he caught himself and kept running, right toward me and right toward the crowd from the Lodge. Ian was halfway between the stockade and the van and shot the running man, who fell to the ground, dropping the rifle.

Ian ran past the van, without a glance at me, shouting at the crowd, "Get back, you fools. Do you want to get killed?" To the United Nations troops, who had also taken cover beside the copter, he said, "Get these people back to the lodge. Paddy's men have the situation covered in the stockade."

Some of the lodge visitors had thrown themselves to the ground, and now got up and walked ahead of the United Nations troops, like sheep being herded into a pen.

When he saw that the gawkers would be safe, Ian walked back past me, not stopping to talk. He gave me a short wave and dropped into a crouch, as a second gunman came out of the stockade. He was a policeman now, not a tourist nor a husband who was worried for his wife's safety. He had a job to finish.

A second African also tried coming out with a weapon. He knew how to use his rifle, and so did Paddy. The moment the smuggler peered out of the gate and lifted the rifle to a firing position, Paddy shot him. He signaled to one of his troops to move the body out of the way, and as they did, a third man came out. He had no weapon, but he tried to escape back into the woods.

"Stop him!" Joseph shouted to the troops on his side of the stockade. "Try not to kill him. Just bring him down so we can question him later."

An African came out next, meekly holding his hands in the air, no weapon. One of Paddy's men stepped forward and handcuffed him, pointing to where he was to sit on the grass. "If you try to run, I'll shoot you," the policeman threatened. The smuggler's eyes rolled fearfully, so I could see only the whites against his black skin.

"How many more inside?" Paddy asked in Swahili.

"Five," the prisoner said.

Paddy went closer to the stockade gate and called out, "Come out, all of you. I'm going to count to ten and if you're not all out, I'm throwing in tear gas. If that doesn't bring you out, I have a grenade left over from the war." He started counting, and he'd only gotten to three, when an African, blubbering incoherently, suddenly fell to his feet, shot in the back by someone inside. "In cages," he said, as his last words.

Two of Paddy's troops came out to move the body, as Paddy continued counting in a calm, male voice.

I heard the words with dread. Only two more in cages. Marcello? Was he armed, or one of the men in cages?

"We're coming out," an African voice called.

The gate swung open again and they came out. The one in front was Marcello. A large, beefy African, dressed in a uniform bedecked with medals, held Marcello fast against him with one arm. His other hand held a pistol that touched the back of Marcello's head. "Let me go or I'll shoot him," he said, in a cold steely voice.

"Go ahead and shoot him," Paddy said. "I don't care. It will just save me the trouble."

Marcello's captor looked puzzled. He obviously had not expected this response.

I jammed Phillip's pistol into my purse and started to run toward Marcello.

I'd only gone two steps, when Ian ran and grabbed me. "Stay back! Marcello is not worth risking your life for." The cameraman had finally gotten past his terror and stepped around Joseph to take a photo of Marcello and his captor. At the same time, one of the bravest of Paddy's policemen had been creeping along the side of the stockade. He stepped around to the front, dropped into a crouch and shot the man in the leg, then jumped to his feet, ready to shoot again.

The gun flew from the big man's hand, as he dropped to his knees, clutching his trouser leg where blood was rapidly soaking through.

"Take him!" Paddy commanded, and two of his men ran to do his bidding. They knew what to do. They rolled him onto his stomach, his hands behind him, and snapped on the cuffs.

"I'm bleeding! I'll die unless you get me some help," the captive said.

"That would solve our transport problem a bit," Paddy observed, "but I think you'll live, more's the pity." He stepped aside to let the photographer take a picture.

Marcello stood uncertainly for a moment, and then he saw me and started toward me. Ian released my arm. "Go ahead. I promised you could talk to him. I sure would like to shoot him. Just say what you want to say to him before we arrest him." He turned toward Marcello. "Stop right there, Marcello, or I will shoot you for trying to escape."

Marcello stopped and said, "Why would I need to escape now? You have come to rescue me, Cara Mia."

"No I haven't, Marcello," I said. "I came to get the truth from you." I hardly recognized the charming, immaculate man I had known in this bedraggled, dirty person. He stepped toward me, and I stepped back.

"I know I stink," he said. "I have been locked up in a cage like a pig going to market. They told me they would give me my share of money today, but they planned to kill me." Smiling at me, he said, "You love me just this much." He held out his hand, his finger and thumb about an inch apart. "After I have had a bath and some clean clothes, I will be once more the charming Marcello you want."

How could he be so cheerful? Didn't he know he had just escaped death and was soon to be arrested and taken to prison along with the other smugglers? But before they took him away, I had to know. "Why did you kill Phillip?"

His mouth flew open and he shook his head. "Who told you such a lie?" He was still smiling, holding up one hand to me.

Ian stepped forward and said, "We have evidence to convict you."

"He was going to turn me in," Marcello responded.

There was no more doubt. He had just admitted to killing Phillip. I felt as if a knife had been thrust into my gut and twisted. The man who had brought me gifts and flowers, and taken me to dinner and danced with me—and even kissed me—was a murderer.

142

"You would have been better off if you let him turn you in, and you had revealed the plan. You'd be a hero," Ian said. "With all the time and effort you put into this plan, all the people who had to be recruited, and all the risks you and other people have taken, you end up with nothing." Ian turned to Paddy. "Do you want to do the honors, Paddy, or shall I?"

"I'll do the part for Uganda and you take over the rest, my boy," Paddy said, and turned toward his men. "You chappies can keep on with the cleanup and tagging process for a few moments, and I'm sure the photographer would like a few more photos." He closed the few steps between us and said to Marcello, "In the name of her Majesty the Queen, the Prime Minister of Uganda, and what's left of the government of the Congo, I am arresting you on charges of smuggling. Other charges may follow."

Marcello said nothing and his pleased expression didn't change. It was as if this was playacting and he would not be found guilty of anything.

Ian took Paddy's place. "In the name of her Majesty the Queen, the Prime Minister of Kenya, and the authorities of Interpol, I am arresting you on charges of smuggling and murder and such other charges as may later apply. Joseph, hand me the handcuffs."

Marcello grabbed my hand and jerked me along with him as he moved toward the lake, where a boat stood idling at the pier. In the moment when his captor was being shot in the leg, Marcello had grabbed his captor's gun and now held it to my head. "You must come with me. I did this for you." A shot from Ian's pistol narrowly missed me as it struck Marcello's arm. He cursed and returned fire twice in rapid succession, the first bullet missing Ian, the second striking him in the arm.

"Let me go, Marcello," I begged. "I'll give you some money. You need money wherever you going."

He's crazy, I thought, *and I have got to humor him. Once I get on that boat I'm done for. Even now Ian and Joseph are afraid to shoot at him for fear they'll hit me instead.* I dug in my heels as much as I could in the gravel of the Murram road. Marcello was slowing and gasping for breath, and I realized that he probably hadn't had food or water for two days, but he still had a firm grip around my waist.

""Give me your money," he said.

"My purse is zipped and you're holding me so tight I can't reach it."

He eased his hold for just a moment, and I slid the purse far enough down to reach my wallet. He grabbed for it, but I hurled it back toward Ian and Joseph.

"Bitch!" he snarled, and backhanded me so hard that everything went black. Before I could move, he grabbed me up again. Neither Brian nor Ian dared to shoot him, as he held me close to him, but I was slowing down his attempt to escape.

I was stunned by what happened next. I saw a little girl in a pink dress and sun bonnet running from her mother up toward the road that led to the lake. "Wait, Marigold!" her mother called. "Come back!"

"The nice soldier said I could ride in the helicopter," she called.

"He meant you could ride some other time, Marigold. They are busy now with the bad men."

I was amazed at how calm the child's mother was under the circumstances, and what a quick thinker she was. I guessed instantly what was going to happen next.

Marcello released me, darted over and grabbed up the child as quickly and gracefully as if he'd been practicing it. If Ian and Joseph had been unwilling to shoot because of me, they were even less likely to do so with a small child being held as a hostage. She kicked against him, and clawed at him screaming, "You're hurting me! You're a bad man!"

Marcello ran with her. He could make better time now, because she was not as heavy as I was. Then the little girl sank her teeth into his arm, and he cursed and flung her aside, running freely in a zigzag pattern toward the pier.

He was farther away now than he had been with either hostage.

"Shoot him!" Ian shouted. " You're closer than I am."

I pulled the pistol from my purse and aimed it at Marcello. I couldn't shoot him in the back no matter what he'd done. As if he were reading my mind, Marcello paused, turned around, and stood for a moment, taking one last look at me before he left for good. *Phillip's pistol will get Phillip's revenge*, I thought, and pulled the trigger. A bullet struck Marcello in the shoulder, and I saw blood spurt from him, as he turned and kept going, running across the pier, climbing down the steps and into the boat. In a moment, he had backed the boat out and turned it into the lake. As the vessel moved, Marcello slumped over the wheel, and the boat began making huge circles in the water.

I didn't know where he was going. I never expected to shoot another human being, but I had shot him.

The mother of the little girl scooped up her daughter, and squeezed her so hard with relief that the child said, "Mama you're hurting me just a little. I know you told me not to bite people, but the mean man was hurting me."

"You did the right thing this time, Marigold, and I'm proud of you."

I saw the photographer approaching, and, as I stepped aside, he took photos of the circling boat that was leaving a trail through the placid water of the lake. Then, he turned to interview the mother and little girl.

Ian ran toward me, and I saw that his left arm was hanging limply and his shirt sleeve was soaked with blood. With his good arm he pulled me against his chest. "Did he hurt you?" he asked. "I saw how he got you."

"I'm all right, Ian. He hurt you more. You'll need a doctor."

"I'll soon have one."

"What happens to everybody now?" I asked, walking with him back toward the van.

"The wounded, including us, will be taken to the hospital in Kasese by the United Nations boys. A lorry has been sent to haul away the dead bodies and those big shipping crates, which, by the way, I think have coffins inside them. Paddy is having the place stripped and searched, including the shipping boxes and coffins. The police Rover from Kasese will take their own troops back home, plus the two who are presently cuffed and taped in the back of the van."

"We found something, sir," called one of Paddy's troops from the top coffin. "There's a body in here. The planks underneath are kind of loose, and there's some gold in there, and what looks like a lot of English shillings and Belgian Francs."

"Well done!" Paddy called back. "Do you think you can move the top box so you can search underneath it for the others?"

"Well, sir, it won't hurt this body when we push the box down, and then you can get to what is underneath. When the lorry comes, they can load up all the coffins." The top box was tipped and slid down, tumbling to one side as it hit the ground. The second and third also were searched for treasure. Paddy exclaimed, "What a find! This is a glorious end to a long career of mine. Nobody else that I know of found anything like this. Well, maybe the Nazis, but nobody out here in Africa."

The photographer finished filming the two Africans in cages, and they were put on the helicopter to go to the hospital as well.

As Ian and I climbed aboard the United Nations helicopter and took a seat, I asked, "What happens next? They need to get the treasure in a bank vault tonight."

"Paddy will get as much as he can into his helicopter. It doesn't take up much space, but it's very heavy, so some of it will have to go in our little safari van. It got dinged up with shots, but Joseph thinks he can get it safely back to Kampala."

I couldn't ask Ian anything more right then, because we had to put on our ear muffs to mute the noise of the helicopter.

As we lifted off, I looked down at the lake. I saw the boat still circling, but it looked empty. Where was Marcello?

Chapter 22

Later, we went to the hospital to see Charlie. The small facility was overflowing with the injured smugglers, as well as the injured policeman and Charlie, and Ian, who had his left arm in a sling. So much had been happening at the lake that, although I had seen a bullet hit him, it had not really registered. The doctors had taken him in ahead of the smugglers, removing the bullet from his forearm and setting the break.

Charlie sat propped up in bed, bandages across his bare chest and crisscrossing his head. What I could see of his face was a mass of purple bruises, and one eye was swollen shut. He, too, had his left arm in a sling, and the hand on that side was so swollen he couldn't close it. Two fingers were broken and had been splinted. "It looks worse than it is," he said, "and that's saying a lot. My jaw is broken, so I can't chew, and the nurses have to feed me soft things like mashed potatoes in small doses and give me liquids through a straw. Hell of a way for a man to eat, isn't it? I've got ribs broken on both sides, and I'm taped up so it hurts to laugh, but there's not much to laugh at right now."

Ian reached out and took Charlie's right hand in his. "You'll be glad to know that the description you were able to give police before they took you into surgery led to the arrest of the head smuggler. Since his activities were in Uganda, he'll face the court in Kampala, and so will all the others that we arrested."

"Lusty?" he asked.

Ian shook his head, as I reached out to touch Charlie's hand next to Ian's. "Lusty didn't make it," Ian said. "I'm sorry. He was a brave dog. He saved your life, and scratched up one of the thugs that attacked you badly enough that we were able to get information out of him on the threat of having Lusty scratch him on his balls."

I saw tears trickle down Charlie's face, but his body shook, and I realized he was both laughing and crying. "Lusty belonged in Africa. He would have hated being in quarantine for six months in Britain. He was used to being with me all the time. When I get back to the UK, I'll get me a puppy, and maybe a wife, if I can find one who would like a grizzled old man with a puppy to train."

"I'm sure there will be women enough in the UK who would love to be your wife," I said.

"My money will help my case," he said. "How about you?"

"She's my wife," Ian said

"Oh come off it!" Charlie said. "You're pretending just as you are pretending to be tourists. How long do I need to keep on referring to you as Mr. and Mrs. Warner?"

"You can stop that right now. And tomorrow, or the next day, we'll be leaving and going where people know us," Ian said.

"Can you have Lusty cremated?" Charlie asked. "That way, I can take him with me without any quarantine time."

"Of course," Ian said. "I'll take care of everything. As soon as you're able, I'll have you airlifted to Nairobi."

"Did the UN fellas get all the information out of you that they wanted?"

Charley's face twisted into what I took as a smile. "I told them enough to get me a good-sized piece of a Swiss bank account and to put some copper company management behind bars."

"You will probably get a reward from the Uganda police and maybe even a award from the Queen," Ian said. "I think there'll be a ceremony to thank you, probably making you an honorary member of the police, with a bit of a financial reward for helping us recover so much of the treasury."

Charlie raised his hand and waved it feebly across in front of him. "No public ceremonies until you're sure you've rounded up all the smugglers. I can't take another beating in an alley."

"The police have been busy," said Ian, "and the jails are full. The smugglers are trying to get out of the country like rats jumping off a sinking ship."

Charlie talked slowly, his lips so swollen I had difficulty hearing all he said, but he kept going. "If I can't find me a suitable wife who's willing to hear all my adventures, I'll look for a men's club where I can sit around with the other old duffers and natter on about what we did when we were young."

"You'll have way more adventures to talk about than the others," Ian said. "And you won't have to exaggerate. They will probably be bragging that they knew all along that Churchill was right. You'll have the advantage of having a certificate of commendation to back up your story." He stood and leaned over to give Charlie's good shoulder a slight squeeze. "We'd better go, and give you a chance to get some rest. I've arranged to have trustworthy police stationed just outside your door to make sure no avengers turn up."

I stood, too, and bent over to kiss Charlie on a portion of his forehead that was not bandaged and was almost a normal color. Then I walked out beside Ian, eager to escape from the hospital. I'd seen enough blood and injury, and, although I couldn't erase the images that swarmed through my mind, at least I could leave the reality of it behind.

151

Ian said nothing until we were outside in the sunshine. People went about their business: women carrying bulging mesh bags from shopping expeditions; men discussing a rugby match, or driving through the street in a Mercedes, unaware of all that had happened that day, for it had not happened to them.

"Care for some dinner?" Ian asked.

"Dinner?" I didn't know what time it was, and it seemed that days had passed since morning, not just hours. Shadows were long on the pavement, and the sun beyond the towering mountains put them in dark silhouette. I felt empty, and not hungry for food, but I would eat and try to make myself get back to normal. We had had no lunch, and had not given a thought to it, but it was dinner time now. "Yes," I said, and let Ian lead me down the street to the hotel.

As we entered the lobby, I saw how well-dressed the people were, and I realized how filthy and disheveled we looked. We certainly didn't look like average tourists. We both had blood spatters on our clothing, Ian's shirt sleeve had been cut off by the doctors to treat the bullet wound, and debris from the helicopter backwash clung to our hair. "We need to clean up," I said. "Looking like this we might get turned away by the dining room."

"I'll need your help bathing and dressing." Ian said.

I hadn't even thought how filthy and disheveled we were, and how the other diners must have regarded us. But this was East Africa, and travelers often showed up covered in dust.

In the room, I unbuttoned Ian's shirt, and he took his right arm out of the sleeve and lifted it around to the other arm. The doctors had slit the sleeve to allow for the cast on Ian's arm. I replaced the sling, and he put his right hand on the chair arm to help himself up. Without my help, he got out of his shorts and underpants, letting them lie on the floor. I watched him walk to the bathroom, keeping two steps behind him. Even bruised and bandaged, his body was as handsome and muscular as one of Michelangelo's statues. I ran water in the bathtub and helped him in.

"I'll need you to give me a good scrub," he said. When I hesitated, he said, "I'm not embarrassed to be asking for help. Everybody needs help sometime. You're not bothered by my nakedness, are you? You must have seen Phillip's body. Just don't be comparing me with anyone else."

I had been studying him, wanting to touch him, to kiss him, and maybe to cry against his shoulder, but his remark broke my spell of longing. Making sure his injured arm would not get wet, I knelt beside the tub, soaped up a washcloth and began to scrub his back.

After a while, he said, "I think I can manage the rest, but I'll need you to dry me off."

I went back into the bedroom, stripped off my own filthy clothing, and was ready to dry him off.

I took my own turn in the bath, sliding down into the water until it came up to my shoulders, and soaking until it grew tepid.

Half an hour later, we emerged clean and dressed in fresh clothing. No one would guess that we had participated in a bloody afternoon of international police work. If anyone asked Ian about his injured left arm, we could always say it was a hunting accident, and make up a story to fit. He was good at pretending.

We were seated on the veranda, with a view across the hills. Ian laid his right hand on mine. "The usual, my dear?" he asked, and, when I nodded, he ordered gin and tonics for us both. As we sipped our drinks, we watched the sunset, while we waited in silence for our dinner to be served. Even with only one drink, I drank that one too fast, and the gin hit my empty stomach and made the world about me whirl. Everything went black for a moment, and I heard Ian ask, "Are you all right?" But I couldn't reply.

"No," I whispered, feeling so queasy I thought I might vomit.

Ian must have thought the same thing, for he pulled my drink, my plate, and cutlery across the table and out of my reach, and tore off a chunk of bread, thrusting it toward me. "Eat this," he commanded. I took it and put it in my mouth. At first, it seemed to stick in my throat, but then went down and stayed down. Ian tore off more of the bread, and I ate it obediently, and by the time the waiter brought our soup, I knew I would be all right—or, at least, as all right as I could be after what had happened.

"I can manage the soup," Ian said, but I'll need you to cut up the rest of my dinner into small pieces. Tearing that bread was the height of my accomplishments this evening."

Neither of us finished our drinks, concentrating instead on dinner. As it turned out, there was little to cut in our dinner. The pork roast had been cooked until it was falling apart, the steamed marrow was cut into chunks, and the Brussels sprouts were small. We finished up with a cheese course and papaya slices so ripe they could be cut and speared with a fork.

On our way back to the room, Ian said, "I'll need your help again."

"Of course. If the tables were turned, I would do the same for you—gladly."

There was a twinkle in his eye at the last word. "It will only be undressing," he said. "I can sleep naked, or sleep in these clothes. I'll be docile tonight, and likely for the next week, but after that, I intend to pursue you."

"I won't be easy to catch," I said. "I have a lot to get over."

"And unless you decide to leave Kenya early, I have a year to help you get over it"

When I came back into the bedroom, I thought at first that he was asleep, but he opened his eyes and looked at me, reaching for my hand with his right hand.

The moment I got into bed, he wrapped his right arm around me and pulled me against him.

For a moment, I responded to him, but then drew back, riddled with reluctance and guilt. I knew that I had reveled in the sight and touch of him, and it had communicated itself to him.

After a moment, I pulled back even more. "I just want comfort, and reassurance that all this madness and violence is over, and that my life will be normal, and I'll be happy again."

"I can comfort you," Ian promised, "and I'm a good listener if you want to talk, but nobody can promise that things will always be what we consider normal, or that you will always be happy. I think it's fairly certain that the smuggling business and the violence that went along with it are over."

"But not in my mind," I said. "I keep thinking back to all that happened by the lake. I may have fired the shot that killed Marcello."

"And you may *not* have," Ian countered. "He may not be dead, but very likely he is. You only shot at him once. I shot twice, and I think Joseph took a shot at him, and possibly one of the other African policemen did, too. So, your chances are only one in four or five. That's why we have firing squads instead of a single executioner. No one knows for certain whose shot was the fatal one, and therefore no one needs to feel guilty of killing someone."

"But I wanted to kill him," I whispered.

"I'd say that's a normal reaction, and I'm glad to hear you admit it, but he brought it on himself. It was inevitable once he joined the smugglers. They weren't going to let him leave alive whether we came or not."

"He never admitted that he killed Phillip, but when you said you had evidence and that Phillip had called you, I saw the guilt in his eyes. And then he used me for a shield. He would have let me be killed so he could get away. I've been such a fool."

"You're an honest person, Joanna, and so you assume that others are also honest. That makes you easy for a devious man to manipulate. If you were inclined to crime, you'd have suspected him long ago. Forgive yourself and let your heart heal," Ian said.

"I *was* healing, but the violence I have seen has started up the aching all over again. What if I can't get it out of my mind?"

Ian responded," You will. You are a strong woman."

"When Phillip died, his mother gave me a short poem that she said had helped her through the war. I can't remember it all but the title was 'Let Evening Come'".

"That's a good image. Violence and death happen everywhere to all of us sooner or later. You have had more than your share. You can't go back and change any of it. If you had not come to Africa and married Phillip, Marcello would probably still have killed him. Think of the joy Phillip had with you. Someday your heart will have healed and you will be ready to share joy again. You can't make it happen anymore than you can hold back evening and nightfall."

Chapter 23

Over breakfast the next morning, Ian was studying me as we made our way through the usual menu. Finally, when I was sipping my second cup of coffee, he pushed his plate aside and said, "We have some decisions to make."

"That sounds ominous," I said, meeting his gaze.

"Do you want to stay on and have a real safari, or do you want to go home? I think I know your answer, but I'm giving you a chance to decide."

"Go home," I said instantly. "Your job here is finished, so you don't need me anymore. This is a beautiful country, but I need some time away from here before I can get the violent images of what happened out of my mind."

He laid his hand over mine. "Try to remember the good bits."

"There *were* some good moments," I admitted. "There were good parts—the the quiet times with you, seeing the elephants, the hotel gardens, and the sunset beyond the mountains."

"Perhaps we can have some good times in a different setting later," he suggested. "Right now, I've got to make a few phone calls.

He stood, dropped his napkin beside his plate, and touched my shoulder. "You'll be all right here?"

"If you're sure the smugglers have all been rounded up."

"Just to be on the safe side, a policeman is standing guard just over there, watching every movement." He pointed to an African clad in the traditional white *kanzu* that I'd seen so often on hotel waiters.

He was back in a few minutes. "If Charlie is able to travel, the three of us can fly out late this afternoon—unless you'd rather go back to Kampala in the safari van," he concluded wickedly.

"I didn't think it was even usable, after the bullets struck it."

"It's a tough little vehicle. Joseph had some difficulty in getting it to a garage with two flat tires, and the gas tank had taken a hit and was leaking, but all that's been taken care of. Joseph would like to have it—with a new paint job—and I think we can arrange it."

Charlie was sitting up in bed, allowing a nurse to feed him, although I knew that at least one of his arms was in good working order. We waited until he had finished his breakfast before Ian began talking.

"When do you think you'll be well enough to leave the hospital?" Ian asked.

"As soon as the doctor discharges me, and, if it's not soon, I'll sign myself out and take my chances. I'm not used to having nursing sisters come around every hour, taking my temperature, checking my bandages, and asking me how I feel."

"Lusty's ashes won't be available until tomorrow," Ian said, "but I can arrange to have someone pick them up and put them on the next plane."

"Can you? I don't want to impose on Toby and his wife, but maybe I can find a little place in Nairobi. Maybe even stay at the Norfolk, or the new Stanley until I can get a ship to Southampton."

"Are you planning on staying in Kampala, or going on to Kenya? The copper company has a plane that may be flying out later today, and it may or may not have space for three passengers. East African airways has a regular flight that goes tomorrow. If we can't get on either of those, I can summon the helicopter. Paddy wants us to use it as much as possible. Nobody around the station knows how to repair it, so when it begins to need spare parts, it'll be junk."

"I'll be ready whenever you say," Charlie said. "But you've got to go get me some clothes. My new gentlemen suit is bloodied and torn, and the trousers were split open to get them off me quickly. I need something besides this hospital gown to cover my bum. It's the only part of me that didn't get bruised and bloodied, but I don't like parading it around."

Ian and I both laughed, and I said we would go take a look at the thrift shop where he'd found his gentlemen suit.

SOON AFTER, IAN AND I stood examining clothing at the crowded little thrift store. "These clothes come in by the bale," Ian said. "Mostly things that didn't sell in your thrift shops."

"You mean *American* thrift shops. It's no wonder most of these didn't sell. I question why anyone bought some of these in the first place. Oh, look! A Nehru jacket. That's been out of style for about twenty years, and wasn't in style more than a few months even then." I held up the blue jacket with a high standup collar and buttons all the way down the front

"It may be a bit snug for Charlie, but he could leave it un-buttoned," laughed Ian. "Here's a pair of khaki trousers with turned-up cuffs that might fit. Now, find him a shirt. Do you think he'd wear this flowered Hawaiian one?"

I laughed. "The color goes well with the Nehru jacket. Let's take it. Here's another memento from the past, a poodle skirt. I had one a lot like this when I was fourteen, or fifteen."

"And I'll bet you looked cute in it," he said.

159

I realized we were laughing together, at least for a few moments, putting the horror behind us.

I held up another garment, a pencil-thin skirt that came down about to my ankles, and had a slit up the back that would have hit me mid-thigh, and I pointed out some plaid shorty pajamas for Charlie.

We looked at a few more on items and then paid for Charlie's clothes. I knew I looked bedraggled, but I was too tired to care about my appearance. When we got back to the hotel, the African woman who made up our room came out bearing our Safari clothes in her hands. We'd dropped them in the large trashcan beside the dresser.

"I wash them for you?" she asked. "Ready in four hours." She held up four fingers.

I shook my head, "No. For you." I pointed from the clothes to her.

"I go to manager to get signature paper *Memsahib*," she said. She smiled and exposed teeth filed to a point. She was back in a few minutes with the clothes in her hand and a piece of paper which she handed to me.

The manager had written a note asking if I intended to discard the clothing. I wrote "yes," signed it, and gave it back to her. *Asante Sama*, she said.

So much had happened that I had lost my Swahili for a moment. I couldn't recall how to say, "You are welcome." So, I just bowed and smiled as she left.

"That should take care of it," Ian concluded. "Hotel managers here are trying to assure tourists that nothing will be stolen. They can't understand why we would discard perfectly good clothing that only needs to be laundered."

"It would bring back bad memories every time I wore it," I said. "Besides, the shirt was too big."

Ian laughed. "And mine had to be buttoned. Without you to dress me, I'm going to have my houseboy take care of that. I'll miss you, for that and a lot more."

"I'll miss you too, but evening has come for me. Even nights can be long."

"But after all the darkness you have been through, morning will surely come again for you," he said. "You'll be alright."

I smiled. We still had some time together, but this sounded as if he was saying goodbye to me.

Chapter 24

That afternoon, at his insistence, Charlie was released from the hospital with dire warnings from the doctors. Ian had booked a small plane for the three of us, and It sat idling on the tarmac. Charlie went out to the plane in a wheelchair, resplendent in his cast-off trousers and red print shirt with the Nehru jacket draped over his shoulders. The pilot helped Charlie into the plane and handed him the tattered old briefcase that held the ledger and notebook, which Charlie placed on his lap.

The pilot asked, "Are you all right sitting up? We have room enough for you to lie down."

"I want to see this part of Africa for the last time," Charlie said, "and I want to be sitting upright like a man, not lying helplessly like an invalid."

I climbed into the plane tossing our bags behind us. Ian waved to the wheelchair attendant, who turned and walked away. With the pilot's help, Ian climbed in beside me, and the pilot slammed the door. In a moment, we were racing across the tarmac, then lifting into the clear sky.

The plane flew low, and I spent the flight looking down as Charlie was doing, trying not to think of what I had seen. It was a joy to see elephants below me, looking like huge gray boulders. I thought about the elephant that had saved our lives, and I hoped he was still alive, evading the poachers.

Then, on the twisted ribbon of the road, I spotted a lorry carrying what looked like a coffin. I leaned across the aisle and told Ian. He saw it as well. "It may be nothing," he said. "Just some poor sod who has died in Africa. Or it may be one of the smugglers' coffins, prepared and hidden away before we got to their headquarters. We'll get to Entebbe well ahead of the lorry, and if Joseph or the Rangers haven't spotted it and stopped it, I'll contact Paddy. It won't leave the country, for sure, not without our taking a good look at what's inside."

We lapsed into silence, and, while my eyes were taking in the scenery below me, my mind's eye kept seeing the curving wake of Marcello's boat, his body slumped against the wheel. I hadn't seen the boat capsize, but I imagined it happening. I saw the faces of the evil smugglers, and the line of coffins beside the stockade. I heard again the cracks of bullets from rifles and pistols, and the shattering of glass as our safari van was hit.

Then I was seeing the shining expanse of Lake Victoria, and our plane came down onto the runway at Entebbe, cruised to the end of the tarmac, turned and made its way slowly back toward the terminal.

We had little luggage. I carried it, since I was the only one of our trio who had not been injured. Charlie had his passport and bankbook in his pocket, and carried his briefcase with his precious ledger and notebook full of Congolese copper mine records. He patted the ledger and said with satisfaction, "I'm not leaving this behind, as far as I have brought it. It's my guarantee for my safety and money."

Paddy met us, slapping us all on the back and congratulating us for taking down the smugglers. He was in charge of arrangements in Uganda, but Ian was the boss over all of it, from offices in Nairobi, and none of us mentioned Charlie's ledger and notebook, as Ian would be the one to follow up on the Swiss Bank accounts and copper mine records.

But Paddy had news for us about the smugglers, and talked as he found seats for us in the terminal.   "The

Congolese are in the hospital, and three are in jail here, including the bloody European who contacted Charlie, who keeps screaming his head off. One minute he keeps claiming that he needs to see his consul, and the next minute he's claiming he has British citizenship, but he can't prove any of who he is. I don't know how in hell he planned to eventually get the loot and leave the country, but we've solved that for him now. As soon as we can arrange it, we can have a hearing and get all the information we can out of him. Than we can turn him over to Interpol."

Paddy paused and then said, looking at Charlie, " Bless me, I haven't even been introduced to you. Patrick O'Rourke." He stuck out his hand.

"Charlie Hill, resident of the Congo, but I have a British passport." He took it out so Paddy could see it, but didn't open it, and I suspected it might be expired. "I also have sufficient funds so that I will not become a public charge, and I plan to move on to Kenya as soon as I can, and leave Africa altogether, as soon as I'm well enough to travel." He displayed his bank book as well, and then put away both documents.

"Charlie has been invaluable to us," Ian said, "and he was damn near killed in helping us. I want an official commendation for him, if you can arrange it, and transportation to Nairobi."

"That brings up my next question," Paddy said. "How would you like to be transported back to Nairobi? It's a little late in the day to arrange for a flight. You can either take the train, which gets you there in the morning, or spend tonight here in a hotel, and fly out tomorrow morning. Either way, you'll get there about the same time. Think it over and discuss it among yourselves." He turned to me. "We questioned Maria Ferretti at some length, and it turns out I'm fairly convinced that she knows nothing about the smuggling operation, only that her lover said he was going to do business with some Congolese businessman and would see her on his return to Kampala. So, all we are charging her with now is attempted murder, since she held you at gunpoint. Do you want to drop the charges — with the possibility of bringing the charges again later — so that we can let her go? For my part, I'd be damned glad to release her. She's really been a pain in the you know what."

"Do whatever you want," I said.

He nodded. " I thought you'd agree, so you won't have to come back to testify, and she won't be needed to give evidence against the smugglers."

"I suppose we could get Ms. Ferretti to identify the body," he said, no longer addressing me, but all three of us. "They found it about noon, today, and it's in a coffin — actually, one that they were intending to ship him out in — and it's on a lorry on its way here. It should arrive in about an hour."

So, the coffin I'd seen on the lorry *was* Marcello's. I felt faint, and waited for Paddy's next statements. Had my bullet killed him?

Chapter 25

Paddy went on, apparently not noticing what I was sure was my suddenly pale face. "The boys who brought in his body said he had three bullet wounds, but he was full of water, so we are putting his death down as drowning."

So, I had not killed Marcello. I was relieved.

"I'd like to take a look in that coffin," Ian said. "If they used any of the coffins the smugglers had, it's ironic that Boehner Mattie is being shipped out just as the smugglers intended he would be. We had a quick look at the three coffins at the stockade, but the helicopter had to leave quickly because of injuries."

"Then would you officially identify the body?" Paddy asked. Ian glanced quickly at me and then back to Paddy. "I can do it if it speeds things up here. Otherwise leave it up to Ms. Ferretti. She certainly knew him better than I did. I only saw him for the few minutes at the stockade."

"Any decision about your travel?" Paddy asked, changing the subject away from Marcello's identification.

Again Ian glanced at me. "Joanna?"

"You two men should decide. Charlie probably is the worst off."

"It's a toss-up for me," Charlie said. "Am I safe while we're traveling? We might as well keep on and not wait until tomorrow. So it's the train. I like trains, and this will be my last chance to take the train in Africa. What about you, Ian?"

"I think it's easier for the police to put us on the train. You know how the government operates. No airplanes when a train will do, and no train when a police lorry will do.

Besides, if we wait until tomorrow morning, that would mean three hotel rooms in addition to the air fare."

So Ian and I were no longer to be sharing a room. I was both disappointed and relieved. I was attracted to him, but I had to ask myself if it was just because he'd been a safe haven in a time of danger. But I was a little miffed that he had so quickly decided not to be close to me anymore. Our charade was over.

Paddy nodded and smiled. "I was hoping you would decide on the train, but after all you've been through, I couldn't insist. Let's go to the station and take care of some paperwork. By that time the coffin should arrive — if that's who it is in the box — and we can put it on the same train. I'll count on you, Ian to make sure it stays in custody of the police. We're sending an *askari* along with the coffin."

Paddy said," Joseph is just outside waiting to take us to the police station."

Joseph was cleaned up and smartly dressed in his police uniform. He and Ian exchanged salutes, and he bowed at me and gave a wide grin. He opened a door to a shiny new van. Before I could ask about the old one, Paddy said, "The other one took so many bullets that Joseph barely got it here. It will be his if he can get it running again."

In the station, Paddy spread out a fresh copy of the *Argus*. "Look at that," he said proudly. On the front page there was a picture of him with the little girl and her mother. There were shots of the lodge, the stockade, and United Nations troops climbing into the helicopter. When the story continued on page three, there were shots of handcuffed Africans being guarded by Joseph. I realized most of the pictures were posed after we left.

"I have copies of the paper for each of you," Paddy O'Rourk said, handing them to us. "There will probably be an article or two of this in the *Standard* as well."

I scanned the rest of the front page, looking for any pictures of Ian and me, and was relieved there were none.

"The article says the treasure was in the millions," I said. "How *many* millions?"

"Money changes value from day to day," Paddy said. "And the gold has to be weighed and priced, so I can't really tell you. I just wish some of it were mine."

Ian responded, "Some of it may be. You should get some kind of reward."

Joseph took us to the train and arranged separate compartments for each of us.

"You men may need some help changing clothes," I said.

"I'm not changing," Charlie stated. "You two didn't buy me anything to change into, and this tomfoolery jacket doesn't even allow for all my bandages. It doesn't even meet, much less button. I'll be sleeping in these clothes, with the jacket as extra cover on the bed."

I laughed, and Ian said, "You have my change of clothing in the suitcase, Joanna, but I won't bother with changing."

Ian had that uncanny ability that some men have of always looking neat. This would probably be the last time I'd see him, so I decided to make myself as presentable as possible with the clothing and toiletries that had survived our harrowing journey.

I was in my compartment looking out, when I saw a coffin being loaded onto the train. It must have been Marcello's, for Ian and an African policeman stood watching as it was lifted off the back of the lorry and into a car that was out of my line of vision. The lorry drove off, and Ian strode back along the tracks past me.

169

By the time the dinner gong sounded, I had sponged off the sweat and dust the best I could in my lavatory basin. I put on my dress, and carried my cardigan over my arm. My ever-present purse hung over my shoulder, and, out of habit, I had it pressed closely to my side. I couldn't do much for my hair, but, after all, Ian had seen it in worse condition.

As we made our way to the dining car, Ian said, "I think we look presentable enough to be given a table, without my having to pull rank and show my badge."

"Would that work?" I asked.

"I'm not sure, and I hope we don't have to find out. We made our way very well as ordinary tourists. We three make a good team."

"Speaking as the third member of this trio, I don't want to be part of anybody's team from now on," Charlie said. "It's too dangerous. Just look at me—taped up like a mummy and wearing these clothes that don't cover half my bandages. I wish you'd rescued at least the jacket of my gentlemen's suit. But, easy come, easy go."

People did stare a bit, and Charlie pirouetted and smiled at the group, and made a little wave like the queen mother's wave. The other diners smiled back sheepishly, and then gave their attention to the menus.

While we were waiting to be served, Ian asked Charlie, "How old is that passport of yours?"

"*Too* old. I'm hoping the high commission in Nairobi can issue me a new one. Otherwise, I may have to return to the UK as a refugee."

Ian and I laughed lightly, and he said, "In that outfit, they'd believe you."

We dined in silence, speaking only to murmur that a certain food item was good. Every time I looked up at Ian, he was looking at me, but we exchanged smiles and nothing more.

That night, I tossed and turned, never getting really comfortable, until it was almost time to get up. I kept thinking about Marcello, lying in a coffin a few cars behind me. I was glad I hadn't been the one who had to identify him, and I didn't want to be present when his coffin was opened at the morgue. I wanted to remember him at his best, smiling and lifting a champagne glass at a restaurant in Nairobi. Instead, I kept remembering the way his face had looked when I accused him of causing Phillips death, and remembering the feel of his arm across my waist as he half dragged me toward the boat in his escape.

Ian said Maria Ferretti had asked if she might claim Marcello's corpse, but she changed her mind when she was told of the cost involved. Instead, it would be taken from the morgue to the cement plant at the Athi river where he worked. His contract of employment covered sending remains to the city and country of one's origin.

I had assumed that Ian would be escorting me all the way home, but over breakfast, he said, "I was able to get through to your neighbors. Either Peter or Muriel will be meeting you." As if reading my mind, he added, "I would have taken you home, but I still have some loose ends to tie up, and a corpse in a coffin to dispose of."

I tried to hide my disappointment, but I'm sure I failed. But I don't know why I had expected anything further from him, despite his loving and suggestive remarks at Kasese.

As I came down the steps of the train, I saw to my right Marcello's coffin being unloaded. I quickly looked away. Despite his protests that he could take a taxi, Charlie was bundled into an ambulance. As the two stretcher bearers carried him past me, he looked up and said, "When I get well enough, I'm going to find you and give you a proper hug and kiss."

171

"I'll count on it," I said.

Ian came up beside me and said, " I hope your long time of distress will soon be over, Joanna. I'll be in touch."

I saw Muriel waving at me, and walked toward her.

"Dearest Joanna, what on earth have you been doing these few days? You must tell me all about it." As she talked, she led me to the car park, and I got in, tossing the suitcase onto the seat behind me.

"Do I sense a romance here?" she asked.

"I don't think so. He said he'd keep in touch, and, from my experience, that's it."

"Maybe not in this case," she said. "I saw the way he looked at you. Never mind." She glanced in the rearview mirror. "I see them unloading a coffin. Do you know whose it is?"

"Marcello's."

"Oh dear. Well, let's get you home. I want to hear all the details of what happened."

Chapter 26

I spent the next few weeks almost in a trance. I was grateful that I had classes to teach, for when I entered the classroom, I had to focus on that day's lesson, and not let my mind drift back to what had happened in Uganda. I think I did my duty at school, but I have little memory of what I said or did during that time.

At first, Muriel pampered and mothered me, inviting me to dinner with them, or bringing over a plate of dinner, or slice of cake she just made, "So you won't have to bother with cooking," although she knew very well that usually my house boy did the cooking. I thanked her, but I had little appetite, and passed many hours sitting on the veranda staring out at the fading sunlight behind the moolah hills, listening to the sad throb of the death drums.

Finally, Muriel grew impatient. One afternoon, she stormed into my house without knocking and said, "This has gone on long enough, Joanna. Stop feeling sorry for yourself. It's not attractive."

"But I—" I began.

She waved a hand to cut off what I might have said, took a seat beside me at the table, and went on. "Do you think you're the first woman in the world who had someone she loved die? During the war, some people lost their whole families, or saw someone blown to bits by a falling bomb—an innocent person who didn't deserve it. Marcello Bonetti wasn't an innocent victim. He deserved to die."

She waited for me to argue with her, but I only nodded. "I know. He killed Phillip, and I didn't want to believe it until the very last. Then I hated him, but at the last, I didn't want to kill him myself. I only shot to keep Marcello from killing Ian or me, or Joseph."

"And what's wrong with that? You're not a natural killer, but when the moment came, you did the right thing, protecting yourself and those good men."

She picked up the little silver bell from the table and rang it, summoning Muyia, my house boy. "*Chai, Tafidali,*" she said, ordering tea.

"*Ndio, Mensahib,*" he said bobbing a little curtsy as he went to do her bidding.

She turned her attention back to me. "I didn't want you to go, God knows, but I admit now that I'm glad you did, after the way it turned out."

"Glad?" The words stuck in my throat, and I felt near tears, remembering. I fumbled in the pocket of my skirt for a tissue. "What's to be glad about?"

"You Americans talk about getting closure. Well, you *got* closure. What if you hadn't gone looking for Marcello, and were summoned to the morgue to identify his body, or maybe just told that he had been killed. Then you'd always wonder if he had killed Phillip, or if that had been some mistake, and you might even blame that nice policeman for killing Marcello, which brings me around to my mission."

"What mission?"

Our tea came, and Muriel waited for me to pour two cups: one with milk for her, and one with just lemon for me, ignoring my trembling hand that made the cups click against the saucers. She left me wondering while she drank her tea and ate two chocolate biscuits Muyia had made. "We are bringing you out of the shadows," she said. Before I could protest, she went on. "Tomorrow morning, I'm taking you to my favorite beauty salon in Nairobi for a haircut and a perm if necessary. You've let yourself go." She lifted my hand and looked at it. "You could do with a manicure as well, and I think you should wear your blue dress with the white trim, and some pearls."

"What am I getting dressed up for?" I asked suspiciously.

"To have lunch with that smashing policeman. You and Phillip were a good couple, but that's over and can't be changed. You have come to hate Marcello, I think—a smuggler and a murderer. But this Ian is perfect for you, and you can't tell me you didn't develop some feelings for him after spending almost a week in his company day and night."

I felt my face go hot, remembering how comfortable and excited I had felt in his arms.

"You don't have to say a word," Muriel said, with a satisfied smirk. "Your face says it all. Now let's get on with it. Do you have any excuse that you might use for getting in touch with him?"

I thought for a moment. "The suitcase has a few of his garments in it, as well as mine. I've never even unpacked it."

"That's perfect. Now, let's open it and wash whatever filthy things it contains. I'll get Muyia to do it. Then give Ian a call and offer to meet him at the Thorn Tree—let's say eleven-thirty. Then he'll offer to buy you a coffee or lunch, and voila!" She threw up her hands in a triumphant gesture, positive that he would behave as she predicted.

And he did.

IAN WAS AT THE THORN TREE ahead of me, seated at a small table for two. He stood when he saw me—tall and trim and smiling—and held my chair for me. When he saw I had the suitcase with me, he took it, but said, "You could have kept it. I won't be needing it anytime soon."

"Neither will I. Just give it to Charlie."

"I'm glad you called," he said. "I was thinking about you."

"You could have called," I said.

"I was giving you time to recover from all you went through. And you seem to have. You look good. Lovely, actually."

"Thank you. So do you. Good, I mean, not lovely."

He laughed. "Can I buy you a quick buffet lunch here? This is my official lunch hour and I don't think people would believe that I'm gathering evidence from you . . ." He paused, and before I could accept, he went on, ". . . or maybe this was just a quick meeting to give me the suitcase and you're having lunch with someone else."

"I accept. Lunch would be nice."

Ian guided me into the dining room. A lavish luncheon, which looked better than anything I'd had in a long time, was spread out before us, or perhaps it just appeared that way because I was with Ian.

At first I was nervous. Then, after a while, I stopped worrying. Whatever happened after this hour, I was enjoying myself, telling him about school, hearing about his job, and his family back home.

Then he asked me, "What did you tell your parents about our escapade?"

"Nothing. I left a short letter for Muriel to mail, telling them that since it was a school holiday, I was taking a short trip and would write them about it when I got back. I doubt if I'll ever tell them, however. They worry enough about me, and the more they know the more they would worry."

He nodded. "I have a better excuse. I tell my mother that most of my job is something I can't talk about, but that it's not as dangerous as the *Mao Mao* were. Of course, when that was going on, I didn't tell her about it."

176

It seemed only a few minutes before we'd finished lunch, when he glanced at his watch and said, "Sorry to say, but I have to get back to the office. Next time, I'll pick a day when we can spend much longer time together."

I hadn't even thought to mention that his arm was out of the cast and sling, until he put both arms around me briefly in a goodbye hug.

I would have to give Muriel all the details of my meeting with Ian — at least, all that I was willing to share.

Ian called in the middle of the following week, to ask if he could come out to the farm for dinner, if he were to bring a bottle of wine and the steaks.

He was due at five on Friday, and, in between teaching and checking up on the coffee plants in the factory, I was in a frenzy to have everything perfect. Muyia had the house sparkling, the garden weeded and trimmed, and had even picked up the stray fallen leaves that fell off the Frangipani by the back door.

Dinner went fine, and Ian told me that Charlie was soon to leave Africa. "He's got his new passport, the container of Lusty's ashes, and had a fine wardrobe made by a Nairobi tailor. He's spending some of the fortune he had stashed away all those years in the Congo. It's safely in the UK, but Barclay's was able to transfer enough to its branch here. He may also get a cut of the money the copper company managers stole. We were able to freeze the account for the time being. Charlie knows the account number, and so may some others. That ledger and notebook are all the proof he needs as to what went on. Our wealthy friend will never need to wear thrift shop clothes again."

177

I laughed. "Whoever would have guessed that about Charlie?"

Chapter 27

The Bissells invited Charlie and the two of us to their farm for a weekend before Charlie left for England.

Early Saturday morning, Ian and I drove up to the Norfolk Hotel to pick up Charlie. A man out front was bent over, looking at an array of boxes and shopping bags surrounding him. As he straightened and passed money to an African who approached with a case of beer, I saw that it was Charlie—a very different Charlie. His hair and beard were trimmed, and he wore well-fitting khaki slacks and an expensive looking cable-knit pullover or jersey, as the Kenyans called it.

Ian and the African loaded the car under Charlie's direction, and Charlie got in the back seat. Ian and I climbed in the front. As Ian drove off, Charlie asked, "Is this outfit suitable for a weekend in the Highlands?"

"You look grand," I said. "I didn't recognize you at first without your cuts and bruises."

The Bissells' farm was high up in the *Kinangop,* where the air was invigorating and the view was glorious. Hilary and Toby rushed out to greet us. After a startled moment, she threw her arms around Charlie. "Just look at you!"

Charlie laughed. "Quite a change from the stinking derelict you brought back to civilization."

As their house servant and Ian unloaded Charlie's gifts, Toby said, "What the hell is all of this? You must have spent a fortune. "You don't know how good it feels to have something to spend money on. I thought Lusty and I would starve to death in that little house in the Congo" Charlie said.

The house was long and low, with a flagstone veranda on one side that faced Mount Longonot, and one on the opposite side facing the garden, pastures full of sheep and cattle, and a burbling stream at the foot of the hill..

Over lunch out on the veranda, when Tony Bissell referred to me as Mrs. Warner, Ian and I exchanged a look and he announced, "We're *not* the Warners, and we're *not* married. It was a ruse for a police investigation, and thanks to you, we met Charlie, and he was immensely helpful."

"Oh, dear," Hilary Bissell said with a sigh. "I put you together in the east bedroom."

"You really fooled us—seemed like you'd been married for a good while, the way you got on," Tony said. "So are you going to make it legal?"

"Maybe," Ian said. "Right now, we both have some unfinished work. But we can share the bedroom. Don't worry, Hilary."

That afternoon, Ian and I climbed up to the top of Mount Longonot and looked down into what had been a volcanic crater, but was now a grassy plain, filled in by nature. I felt, as I often did in Kenya, that I was on top of the world with nothing above me but an immense blue upturned bowl of sky.

It had grown cool when the sun set, and we sat by a softly crackling fire, sipping wine and talking—or mainly listening to Toby talk.

The next morning we were supposed to sleep in, but I was never a late sleeper, and gratefully opened the door to the servant bearing the usual tea tray. I was about to pull on my robe and take my cup of tea down to the lounge, when Ian said from the bed, "Give me a moment and I'll join you."

Eventually, the rest of the household got up, and by late morning we were off to The Brown Trout for a lunch of roast beef and Welsh rarebit—very British and perfectly done.

Charlie paid for everybody's lunch and said the money was part of his reward for his help with the smuggling case.

"Are you sure you didn't clean out one of those Swiss bank accounts?" Toby joked.

Charlie shook his head. "I thought of it. It was very tempting, all that money, but if there's anybody left among the smugglers, and the business of the copper company is settled they might hunt me down. All I want now is a peaceful quiet life in the English countryside."

Ian laughed.

"Besides," added Charlie, "we had the account frozen until the owners of the copper company finish the investigation."

My time with Ian was comfortable and wonderful. We saw as many of the good things of Kenya as we could fit into our schedules. We flew to Malindi and lay on the white sandy beach listening to the murmur of the Indian Ocean, dining afterward in a courtyard lit by lantern.

He proposed in an offhanded way.

"I've been investigating job possibilities in America," he said, over dessert.

"So now you are going to America?"

"Only if you marry me."

"Of course I will!" I said. After a moment, I asked, "But do you think you would be happy in America? I know how you love Kenya."

"But I love you more," he said. "And, I think there are too many bad memories here for you. Here, I might be competing with ghosts."

During the last school holiday that I would have before the final term of my contract, Ian made reservations for us with Ker and Downey Safari. We picked up the basket of provisions in Nairobi and drove through the Masai area to the campsite.

We had a tent for two that zipped closed for privacy, with two cots and two canvas chairs out front, facing Kilimanjaro. At the rear, the tent zipped open to reveal a canvas bathtub, and when I wanted to wash off the dust of the journey, Africans brought cans of hot water for me. At sunset, Kilimanjaro looked like a vast cake with pink icing.

"This is wonderful," I said, in the darkness of the tent.

"But not very romantic or sexy," Ian said. "I can barely reach you, and we definitely can't share a cot." He came across to my cot, knelt and kissed me. "That's a promise of better things to come," he said.

Tea arrived the next morning while it was still dark, and we dressed hastily in our warm sweaters and slacks for a morning game drive

We stood in the back of a Rover, Ian's arm around me, as we drove around the game park in search of animals browsing on grass or hunting other animals. I had never learned the names of all the kinds of antelope, but I enjoyed seeing them standing in a group with their small tails twitching, until finally one or two would look up at us curiously and then scamper off.

Then we saw an elephant, not rampaging and bellowing with grief and anger and seeking revenge, but calmly walking toward an acacia tree to have breakfast. We watched as he pulled down a tree limb with his trunk and drew its branches into his mouth. Sunlight filtering through the trees struck him just right, and I got one of the best photos of all for my

African collection. I could have watched for hours, but the elephant, satisfied, ambled off.

Back at the camp, the chef, in his dark uniform and white hat, squatted by the fire with a skillet that held wonderful smelling bacon, two fried eggs, and pieces of bread. We drank strong, hot coffee from tin mugs as we watched the sun rise over Kilimanjaro.

Everything was perfect, and I told Ian so.

Soon after, Ian told me that the police were giving a small sendoff party for Paddy before he left East Africa, and that Charlie would be included, even though he was not a policeman. "I would invite you, but these things are usually rowdy and unappealing to women. But you can see both of them the following evening at the airport."

So I did, and Joseph was there as well, resplendent in his Chief's uniform. He grinned with a flash of sparkling white teeth, and extended his hand.

"It's good to see you again, *memsahib*," he said. "We had quite an adventure, didn't we? If you ever come back to Uganda with your man, I'll show you around for a real safari."

"I'd be delighted, Joseph, and you are always welcome to my coffee farm as long as I'm here in Kenya."

Paddy looked different. Without the trappings of his uniform and office, he looked very ordinary, like any other Irishman. He shook my hand and said gravely, "If I should ever meet you and Ian again, I hope it will be for a strictly friendly visit with no attendant dangers."

"And I certainly hope so, too," I responded. "Good luck back home in your new life."

"I don't know indeed what I'll really do with myself, but we shall see," he said.

Charlie gave me a big hug and a kiss on the cheek. "You're a brave lass," he said, "and I think you'll even be able to keep your policeman in line. But if he gives you any trouble, you just let me know."

He handed Ian a check

Ian looked down at it. "What the devil is this for, Charlie?" he asked.

"It's the remainder of what I had sent out to Kenya and never managed to spend. It's a wedding gift, and if you don't marry this woman by the end of her contract here, I'm stopping payment on the check. You'll notice it has no date on it. You'll have to fill that in."

"Are you sure you won't need this?" Ian asked.

Charlie shook his head. "I have plenty where that came from, and I feel like I owe it to you two people." He hugged Ian with a slap on the back, and hugged me again.

Charlie and Paddy walked away together, and we waited until we saw them waving from the second-story windows of the terminal.

As we walked back to the car, which was parked near Joseph's van, Ian said, "I'll bet those two old duffers get drunk as coots before the plane lands in London."

TIME FLEW. I WAS BUSY finishing school and planning the wedding, and Ian was getting all the paperwork done for going to America. We went together to the high commission to prove we paid all our taxes due, so we could leave the country.

We were married at the Anglican Cathedral in Nairobi, two days after the end of the school term. Phillip's parents — who had already told me how happy they were that Marcello was out of my life — flew in for the wedding and to make arrangements for selling the farm to Peter and Muriel. I was glad enough to sign over any claims I might have on the coffee farm. I never thought I deserved it anyway, but Phillip's parents said I was part of the family.

Phillip's father gave me away, Muriel was my matron of honor, and Peter served as Ian's best man. When I entered the cathedral, it looked as if half the population of Kenya was attending, including my teaching colleagues—both American and British—and many of the class of my African students who had been with me for two years and whom I referred to as "mine." One of the students caught the bouquet, to many giggles.

Many of Ian's military and police cohorts gave the usual raunchy toasts typical of a British wedding, and then Ian himself rose and read a letter from Charlie:

"Congratulations to you two. I knew you'd marry eventually. I'm getting married on this day myself. I found a sweet woman who was willing to marry an old duffer like me, and she has a dog. Cheerio, mates!"

After all the festivities were over and the toasts given, Ian and I returned to the coffee farm for the first night of our marriage. We lay together in the darkness, listening to sounds from the country club and animals in the pasture between. Then, the drums began—not death drums but drums of joy.

AS MY GRANDDAUGHTER AND I came down the steps from the attic, Ian came in with the mail. "What are you two ladies doing up in the attic?" he asked.

"Grandma's been reminiscing, but I've been sorting things so you'll know what's left to take when you move."

"What all has she been telling you?" he asked, with a glance at me. He took one of the carvings of a bent old man from her, gave it a sniff, and I saw the same expression cross his face that I knew had crossed mine when, I, too, had

185

smelled it earlier in the day. It was the smell of Africa: unforgettable. Our granddaughter was holding the drum under her arm. She set it down on the floor, and Ian began tapping it lightly. "The drum is still taut," he said. "This really brings back memories."

"She told me all about the animals and the neat restaurants, and the beach at the Indian Ocean, and a really special safari. How did you two meet, anyway? Mama never told me."

Ian and I exchanged glances. We wouldn't tell her about the smuggling and the horrors that went along with it. She wouldn't believe it—or, if she did, she wouldn't understand, and we didn't want to bring it up.

"I stopped her for driving too fast and for not having a left rear mirror," Ian said. "That was the luckiest traffic stop I ever made."

We smiled at each other, sharing our secret.

Memories can't be left behind in some distant time and place. They may fade, or be calm or distorted, but a part of them will be with us forever.

Acknowledgments

Because of my fading eyesight, I dictated this book and, between my southern accent, the use of some Swahili, and the programs difficulty in choosing which homonym to use, the manuscript was full of errors, many of them amusing. I wish to thank the following people who made this manuscript more readable: Wendell Bradley, who read the book strictly for the story; my sister, Margaret Hines, who printed out the manuscript, and read it carefully marking all of the hundreds of technical mistakes and commented on scenes that needed further work; my husband, Gerald Liedl, who took Margaret's marked manuscript and corrected all the technical errors and who then typed changes I made and remade as we went through the manuscript numerous times. I owe him deep thanks. And finally, I wish to thank Joe Perrone, Jr who will undoubtedly produce as beautiful a book out of this manuscript as he has done for four of my latest books.

About the Author

Emilee Hines grew up in Virginia and was in graduate school at UNC-Chapel Hill when she was chosen for Teachers for East Africa, a project of the US State Department. She taught two years at a teacher training college in Kenya and traveled widely in the area each holiday opportunity. She has since returned to East Africa for three visits, and, in 2022, she gave her daughter a trip to Kenya. Emilee especially likes elephants, and one of her main charities is the David Sheldrake Foundation for animals, a group that rescues elephants orphaned by poachers and rears them to return to the wild.

She is the author of over 300 short stories and articles, and has 17 books in print on Amazon, as well as seven she has co-authored, which are now out of print.

If you liked this book or any other of her books, please write a short review for Amazon, Good Reads or any of the media platforms. As the Kenyans would say, "*Assante Sana,*" or thanks.

If you would like to comment or get in touch with her here's how:

Emilee Hines Cantieri
333 Thompson St, Apt 323
Hendersonville NC 28792
Email: Emilee214@att.net

www.ingramcontent.com/pod-product-compliance
Lightning Source LLC
Chambersburg PA
CBHW050842180626

46814CB00007B/2581